THE FRIGHTENERS

PETE JOHNSON

Illustrated by David Wyatt

CORGI YEARLING BOOKS

THE FRIGHTENERS
A CORGI YEARLING BOOK : 9780440864370

First publication in Great Britain

PRINTING HISTORY

Corgi Yearling edition published 2001

3 5 7 9 10 8 6 4

Set in 12½/15½ Century Schoolbook
by Falcon Oast Graphic Art, East Hoathly, East Sussex.

Corgi Yearling Books are published by Random House Children's Books,
61–63 Uxbridge Road, London W5 5SA,
A Random House Group Compnay.

Addresses for Random House Group Ltd companies outside the UK
can be found at: www.randomhouse.co.uk
The Random House Group Ltd Reg. No. 954009.

The Random House Group Limited supports The Forest Stewardship
Council (FSC), the leading international forest certification organisation.
All our titles that are printed on Greenpeace approved FSC certified paper
carry the FSC logo. Our paper procurement policy can be found at:
www.rbooks.co.uk/environment.

Mixed Sources
Product group from well-managed
forests and other controlled sources
www.fsc.org Cert no. TT-COC-2139
© 1996 Forest Stewardship Council
FSC

Made and printed in Great Britain by
Cox & Wyman Ltd, Reading, Berkshire

'Leave me alone!' I screamed

a pile of books. I picked up the

and lobbed it at the Frightener. The book

bounced against the wall, then landed on the ground with a heavy thump. But it hadn't touched the Frightener which had just melted into the gloom.

And throwing that book was so stupid. All I'd done was make the Frightener even angrier than it had been before. Now it was hiding somewhere, getting ready to strike again. Only this time it would make straight for me and its vast jaws would spring open . . .

Chapter One

In the middle of the night they came for me.

The first time I only heard them. The next night I saw them, too. I looked into the darkness and there they were.

The Frighteners.

Just writing their name sends a cold chill down my spine. I really hope you never meet them.

So what happened to me? If I live to be a hundred and twenty, I'll remember every detail.

It all began on a freezing cold morning at the beginning of October. The air was like ice. I couldn't stop shivering, but not just with the cold. I was walking into a school I'd never even seen before.

I had to wait outside the office for my form-teacher, Mr Karr. The school smelt of cold fish fingers. And I seemed to be standing there for ages. I kept thinking about my friends at my old school. If only I were still there with them. If only!

And then this bearded man in a multi-coloured jersey whooshed up to me. 'Chloe Storr,' he practically shouted. 'Splendid. Follow me.' We bounded down the corridor. 'I believe you come from London,' he said.

'Yes, that's right,' I gasped, struggling to keep up with him.

'Well, you'll find life in a quiet village very different. I'm sure you'll enjoy it though.' He opened a door and all the chatting stopped. Eyes peered at me from every corner of the room.

Mr Karr warbled on about how it wasn't easy being new, especially in the middle of a term, but he knew they'd all make me feel very welcome.

'Do we have a volunteer to look after Chloe?' he asked

I gave one of my really sickly 'Please like me' smiles. But no-one said anything. One girl at the front smiled at me. All the rest just sat there like a bowl of prunes.

'They're a friendly lot really,' said Mr Karr. 'They're just a bit shy with newcomers. Now, where will you sit?'

At my old school we sat round these big tables which was really friendly. Here they were in rows. And there were only two spare places. One was next to a girl with very long blonde hair near the front, the other was beside a boy sitting at the back by the window. He was the only person not gawping at me. He was frowning at his desk.

'You will sit beside Tanya,' said Mr Karr.

The blonde-haired girl sprang up angrily. 'But she can't. Karen will be back soon.'

'Not until next month,' said Mr Karr, firmly. 'Until then Chloe will sit next to you. I know you will look after her. And Alison, as I've had no volunteers, I'm picking you to look after Chloe at breaktime.'

So I scrambled next to Tanya, giving her the biggest smile I could manage. She didn't smile back, just snapped, 'You know you can only sit there until Karen gets back.'

Talk about friendly! I was getting cross now and muttered, 'And who made you Queen of the World?' I'd only said that under my breath but she must have had supersonic hearing, because she gave this angry flounce and ignored me for the rest of the lesson. She just sat there playing with her hair.

I suppose I ought to tell you that she was very pretty and she had the kind of long blonde hair I've always wanted. My hair is a dull, mousey brown colour. I'm quite short too and have what people call an interesting face which means I'm not wildly attractive (although I'm not a dead-ringer for the Elephant Man either).

Tanya started whispering to this boy in front of us, who kept turning round.

Finally he spoke to me. 'Hello, I'm Tom.'

'And I thought I'd become invisible. Hello, Tom.'

He grinned. 'I bet you support one of the London clubs like . . . West Ham.'

'Right first time,' I said.

He grinned again. Tanya was clearly furious at having the attention taken away from her. She whispered something I couldn't hear. But Tom didn't say another word to me.

I got out my pencil case. It was one of those fluffy ones made of fake fur which were really cool at my last school. I opened it. Inside all my friends had written little messages on it for me. I started reading them again and I felt so lonely. I even gave my pencil case a little stroke just as if it were a tiny pet.

I hardly wrote anything, though. I couldn't. They were way ahead of me in maths. So I sat there in a total fog. At the end of the lesson Mr Karr asked me to stay behind. Everyone else had left for morning break, except that boy who sat by himself at the back. He seemed to be drawing something.

Mr Karr tried explaining where I'd gone wrong. I became more confused than ever. In the end he told me not to worry, I'd soon catch up. But I didn't believe that and I don't think he did either.

He took me out to the playground at the front of the school. I stood there watching some of the boys play football. I felt all nervous and shy. Then a girl came up to me. The one who'd smiled at me in the classroom.

'You're Chloe.'

'Yes.'

'I'm Alison.' She spoke very softly.

'Hi Alison.'

'Are you a cockney?' she asked.

That took me by surprise. 'No, I'm not.'

'Oh, you sound just like one.'

I don't, actually. But I didn't argue with her.

There was silence for a moment as we struggled to think what to say next.

'So are you cooked?' she asked suddenly.

I gaped at her. 'I'm sorry.'

'Are you cooked?'

'I don't think so.'

'You must be packed then.'

I couldn't understand a word she was saying. 'No, I don't think I'm that either,' I said at last.

After another deathly pause she

whispered, 'See you later then.'

'Bye,' I replied. Then all at once I understood what she'd been asking me. 'Alison, I'm having a cooked meal today, so yes, I'm cooked,' I called. 'Sorry for being so dense.'

But she can't have heard me. Some other people did though and gave me funny looks. I crawled back into school.

A group of girls and Tom were standing by the pegs. Tanya was in the centre of them. She had her back to me. She was sniffing her pencil case and saying in this very affected voice, 'Don't you just love my fluffy pencil case everyone. I can't stop looking at it. Isn't it just the most wonderful one you've ever seen in your whole life?'

The girls around her were in hysterics. I wasn't. But then I was the one she was impersonating. And I hadn't been showing off my pencil case at all. I just liked it. They were being totally unfair.

Suddenly Tom spotted me. Then every

face whirled round. And Tanya stopped her impression, her face reddening a little. I never said a word, just slowly walked back to the classroom. That boy at the back was still there. But he didn't even look up when I came in. I sat there seething with hurt and anger.

Then Tanya swept back. A little group, including Tom and Alison, huddled around her. She got out this bag. We weren't allowed to wear trainers to school but she'd sneaked in her new ones to show everyone. I thought I'd die of excitement.

She waved these trainers about and went on and on about how totally wonderful they were. She was such a show-off. And all the time she spoke she had this smug grin on her face. She was setting my teeth on edge.

Then Alison suddenly asked me, 'What do you think of Tanya's new trainers, Chloe?' She was trying to be friendly, draw me into the conversation. But they belonged to that awful, stuck-up girl who'd just done a very cruel impression of me.

So I blurted out, 'Yes, those trainers were quite fashionable in London about three years ago.'

Immediately I wished I hadn't said that. But it was too late. Tanya's face just froze with shock. Then she turned her back on me as Tom snarled, 'You think you're so great coming from London, don't you?'

He didn't understand. I'd only said that to put Tanya in her place.

And then lessons started again and I made a truly massive mistake. Mr Karr asked me to tell the class about where I'd lived before. So I did. And for the first time that day I enjoyed myself.

I told them all about my old school and how it had a swimming pool and big playing fields (unlike this place) and then I got carried away. Soon I was turning my last school into a palace.

After I'd finished there was silence. Even Mr Karr's smile looked a bit frozen. 'Well,' he said, 'I hope you won't find life here too dull, Chloe.'

And as the atmosphere had become

distinctly heavy I replied, all bright and breezy, 'Oh no, this is a really exciting, modern place. I see you've got colour television here now and indoor loos . . .' I was only joking. And I'm always saying daft things like that. Ask any of my old friends.

But no-one smiled. There was lots of angry murmuring, though. And Mr Karr said in this very tight voice, 'Right, well I think we'd better get back to our work now.'

After the lesson finished and Mr Karr had rushed off to see a parent, half the class circled around my desk. You can guess who led the jeering. Yes, Tanya.

'I hate big-headed people who look down on everyone else,' she said.

Hark who's talking I thought. But I never said a word. I'd said far, far too much already. I just shrank into myself while the insults rained down on me. Only the boy at the back didn't join in. He

was slumped so low in his chair he seemed as if he was about to slide off it.

'If your school was so great, what are you doing here?' demanded Tom.

Before I could reply, this voice said, quietly, 'Leave her alone.'

The boy at the back had got to his feet. He was very small and thin, his clothes seemed to just hang off him. He looked as if one gust of wind could blow him over.

'Stop picking on her,' he continued, in the same, low voice. 'You're not giving her a chance.'

I waited for them all to turn on him. But amazingly, they didn't. Instead, they all seemed to freeze. You'd have thought a very scary teacher had just spoken, not this frail-looking boy.

'I expect you're hungry,' he said to me.

I nodded.

'Follow me then.' Not a word was spoken as we walked to the door. Even Tanya was silent. It was incredible.

'Thanks for doing that,' I said to him as we walked along the corridor.

He didn't answer.

'What's your name?' I asked.

He turned to me for a moment. He had straight, fair hair and looked very pale as if he didn't go outside very much. But it was the eyes I noticed most: very large and as blue as the sky on a hot summer's day. They seemed to look right through you.

'My name's Aidan,' he said.

He didn't say another word until we reached the dining hall. There was a queue stretching out of the door. We walked right to the front of it. I waited for people to cry out about us pushing in. But no-one did. Then Aidan made as if to go.

'But aren't you . . .?' I began.

'I never have school dinners. I prefer to eat alone. But you'll be all right now.'

'Yes, thanks – thanks a lot.'

He turned back for a moment. 'About your maths, I could help you catch up, give you some extra coaching.'

I was stunned. 'That's really nice of you,' I began. But he'd already walked off.

In the queue I spotted Alison. 'Yes, I am cooked,' I grinned.

She smiled nervously back.

'I don't think I'm very popular,' I said. 'Some of the class have just been having a right go at me. After one morning they've decided they hate me.'

'We don't get many new people,' replied Alison. 'Most people have lived here all their lives.'

'What about Aidan?'

She looked startled by this question. 'Aidan, well he's quite new too, started about a year ago.'

'He's been really helpful.'

'Has he?' Then suddenly she leant forward and whispered right in my ear, 'Keep on the right side of him. Don't ever argue with him.'

My breath quickened. 'Why?'

Alison's voice was hardly even a whisper now. 'Just be very careful.'

Before I could ask her anything else, she'd gone.

Chapter Two

We moved here because of my dad.

My mum and dad are teachers. So yes,
I get all the silly jokes: when your parents
are cross with you, do they put you in
detention? All that kind of stuff.

My mum is a nursery teacher; my dad
used to be a deputy headmaster. For
months I hardly saw him. Even at
weekends he'd be shut away doing his
paperwork. And if I even breathed outside
his door he'd shout at me and get all
stressed out.

Then one day I came home from school
to find my dad asleep on the sofa with a
rug tucked around him. At first I thought
he had flu or something. But Mum said
Dad was just very, very tired and was

18

having a good rest. Later Mum told me that Dad was having an extra holiday.

This extra holiday went on for months. I'd see Dad pottering about in the garden wearing his jeans and Wallace and Gromit T-shirt (that's my dad's idea of style!) And when he saw me he'd ruffle my hair and chat about what he'd done at home that day. But all the time there was this sad, faraway look on his face. I was getting worried about him. I knew Mum was too.

Then, one afternoon right out of the blue, Mum announced Dad had a new job and we were moving to a 'lovely village' in the country. Dad would just be working part-time at first so he could be at home more. Mum also had found a part-time job at the local nursery. She told me all this in an awful, cheerful voice. I knew she didn't want to leave. Neither did I. But we had to, for Dad's sake.

The house we've moved to is pretty small. I can't fit half my stuff into my new bedroom. In fact, I just about fit into it. But Mum and Dad keep saying how cosy it all is and they make a big deal of breathing in the fresh air and exclaiming how much cleaner it is here. To be honest, I don't notice any difference. I'm not sure

Mum and Dad really do either.

After my first, terrible day at school, Dad was already at home when I got in. 'How did it go? Not too bad, was it?' he asked. And he looked so hopeful, so eager for everything to be brilliant that I couldn't bring myself to tell him the truth.

'Yes, it was OK.'

'And the first day is always the worst.'

Personally I doubted that.

I only told Harvey what had really happened. Harvey is a snow-white rough-haired terrier, with brown patches on his head and ears and the funniest little tail you've ever seen. Every afternoon he waits for me to come home from school. Once when I went round to a friend's house for tea Mum said Harvey became more and more agitated when I didn't come home. Finally he slipped out to try and find me. He was going in the right direction too. But then Mum saw him and brought him back.

He's a brilliant dog.

That night I gave him a bath, just for something to do, really. Then I let him have a sniff around in the front garden.

Suddenly I started in surprise. Someone was standing just outside my house. He seemed to be watching it. Then a figure stepped out of the shadows. I gasped.

'Sorry, I didn't mean to scare you.'

It was Aidan, standing there in this long, black coat. 'You did say you wanted me to help you with your maths,' he said.

'Well, yes,' I stuttered. But I'd assumed he'd meant at breaktime or something. I never imagined him popping up round my house.

'How did you find me?' I asked.

'Not difficult in a village.' His voice tightened. 'We don't have to do this now. I can go right back home again.'

'No, no, don't be silly,' I said.

Then Harvey began sniffing around Aidan. Normally he is very suspicious of any newcomers. For the first couple of hours he'll sit studying them, growling softly in his throat. But he was leaping around Aidan as if they were old friends.

'Now, aren't you great,' said Aidan, patting him. He looked at me. 'You're very lucky having a dog. What's his name?'

'Harvey.'

'A great name.'

Now Harvey was nudging Aidan as if to say, 'Follow me inside.'

My mum and dad liked Aidan too. Especially when they saw the maths book under Aidan's arm. Well, they are teachers. Mum took Aidan's coat and gave us a tray of drinks and chocolate biscuits to take upstairs.

I opened my bedroom door. 'Sorry it's so cramped.'

'Don't worry, I'm used to it. My bedroom's about the size of a kennel,' replied Aidan.

I brought in another chair and we both crouched around this little table. Harvey settled down between us. I felt shy and more than a bit suspicious. Why was Aidan taking all this trouble? He hardly knew me. 'I should warn you, I'm rubbish at maths,' I began.

Aidan ignored this. 'I'll go through all the things we've done this term.'

'I can't wait.'

Aidan began. He was, actually, incredibly patient, and didn't seem to mind when I asked him to explain things over and over again.

And then I noticed something. The

little finger on Aidan's left hand was missing. There was only a stump where his finger should have been. I couldn't help looking. And Aidan saw me.

'My hand's been like that since I was born.'

'I wasn't staring,' I said.

'Yes you were,' he replied, but he didn't say it nastily. 'When I was little I used to tell everyone a werewolf had chased after me. It bit my finger off but I managed to get away before it could eat anything else. At the full moon, though, I always hide away because the werewolf has got a taste for my blood and comes sniffing after me. I can hear him howling outside my house.'

'And people believed that story?'

'Sort of.'

All of a sudden Harvey jumped up on to Aidan's lap.

'You are honoured,' I said. 'He's never done that with a stranger before.'

Aidan started patting Harvey. 'Animals know I like them. Do you know what my favourites are?'

'You'd better say dogs or Harvey will sulk.'

'Yeah, dogs are excellent. But I like cats too, tigers and sharks.'

'Sharks!' I exclaimed.

'I really like their teeth. Bats are another of my favourites.'

'You're joking.'

'No, I'm not. My bedroom's so small that my mum lets me use the attic. It's like my real bedroom now. And at night when I'm working in the attic there's this little window, and bats are always flying up to it and looking in on me.'

'I don't think I'd like that.'

'But you've got nothing to fear from a bat. They're just hamsters with wings. And if they fly into your hair they're only trying to be friendly.'

'I'll take your word for it.'

'Now humans: they're the ones you've got to fear. They can be nasty for no reason. Like the class today. As soon as you walked in they started picking on you.'

'Oh well, I didn't help with my silly jokes. By the way, why is everyone so . . .' I paused.

'So what?' he asked.

24

'Well, when you spoke to the class they seemed almost scared of you.'

Aidan bent down and started patting Harvey again. 'I hadn't noticed.'

'You must have. Then Alison told me to keep on the right side of you and never argue with you.'

Aidan looked up. His face had darkened.

'So, come on,' I said. 'What's your secret? Have you got a really tough, older brother?'

'I haven't got any brothers or sisters.'

'Snap . . . well, then you must be an expert at karate or judo . . . I bet you can flip people over your shoulder, can't you?'

He shook his head. 'But I can stand up for myself.' He said this quite casually, as if he were stating a known fact. And actually, some small, thin people can be quite wiry and tough. I supposed Aidan must be one of them.

'Anyway,' he said, 'that class is not worth talking about. They're a waste of oxygen.' His voice rose. 'Just don't listen to anything they say about me. Will you do that?' He was staring at me now with his piercing blue eyes.

'Aidan, I make up my own mind about people.'

25

He smiled. 'I'm very pleased you've moved here. I knew from the start you were totally different to the rest of them.'

'I'm certainly different from Tanya. Already we're deadly enemies.'

'You can sit next to me tomorrow if you like.'

That took me completely by surprise. 'Oh, right, well anyone's better than Tanya.' Then in case that sounded a bit rude I went on. 'That's nice of you. Thanks.'

He very gently put Harvey down on the bed and got up. 'I'd better go.'

'Thanks again for the maths lesson. Will it take you long to get home?'

'About half an hour if I daydream. Ten minutes if I don't.' He fixed his eyes on me again. 'Remember Chloe, trust no-one in our class but me.'

Chapter Three

Next morning I walked very slowly to school. I just couldn't make my legs go any faster.

Some girls were huddled together by the pegs. Tanya was right in the middle of them whispering away. When I walked past they all stopped talking. So no prizes for guessing who they were pulling to pieces today.

'My fan club meeting again, is it?' I murmured, determined to look as if I didn't care. But I was so upset I opened the wrong door first of all. Then I found my classroom. Aidan was already there.

I sat beside him. There was a buzz of surprise from the other pupils. I guess girls didn't sit next to boys very often. But Aidan didn't seem to have noticed any of this. He was intent on the book he was reading. He didn't even look at me.

I tapped his book. 'Have you noticed there's someone else sitting beside you, because everyone else has?'

He lowered the book. Last night he'd been really friendly. Now his gaze was totally blank. 'Hello Chloe,' he said, then returned to his book.

At breaktime Aidan stayed behind in the classroom. I decided to have another go at making friends. In the playground I heard this horrible noise. It sounded as if a weasel was being strangled. Actually, it was just Tanya laughing. I avoided her and hovered around four other girls from my class. I tried to join in their conversation. They practically ignored me. Then I said something which I thought was quite funny. 'Oh, ha, ha,' said one girl rudely. In the end I slunk away.

At my old school I was known as a good laugh. In fact, Kara, my best friend, had rung last night saying how everyone was missing me and my silly jokes.

Why was it so different here?

Then a teacher appeared and started ringing this really ancient bell. I couldn't stop laughing. Some of the girls saw me. 'That bell must be about a million years old,' I cried. 'And the teacher doesn't look much younger.'

'I suppose your school bell was made of gold and covered in diamonds,' said Tanya meanly.

'No, we didn't have a school bell, we . . .'

But Tanya had already linked arms with another girl. As they walked into the classroom together I heard Tanya say, 'I'm sick of her looking down her nose at us all the time.'

They'd got me all wrong. I wasn't like that. But it seemed there was nothing I could do. They'd made up their minds about me and that was that.

I was very depressed now. Aidan must have noticed because at lunchtime he said I could share his sandwiches if I wanted. There was a very small playground at the back of the school. You weren't allowed to play any ball games there and hardly anyone used it. That's why Aidan liked it. I wasn't very hungry. But he insisted I eat half his sandwiches. He was much friendlier away from the rest of the class.

Then we went for a walk around the school. In the main playground the boys were playing football. They were rushing about knocking into people and yelling at each other. Then the ball came hurtling over towards Aidan. It lay there at his feet. I thought one of the boys would tell Aidan to kick it back.

But instead, Tom called out. 'Don't worry, I'll get it.' He ran over. 'Sorry about that, Aidan,' he murmured, and kicked the ball far away from us.

'They're very keen not to upset you, aren't they?' I said.

'They just know I don't like football,' said Aidan quickly. Shortly afterwards we walked back towards the classroom. He wanted to finish a drawing he was working on. I was about to follow him when Alison sidled over to me.

'Hello,' she said. 'So how are you?'

'Not very well, but thanks for asking.'

She gave a nervous laugh. 'Yesterday I said something to you about Aidan. I told you not to get on the wrong side of him.'

'I remember.'

'Well, I was only joking.'

'Were you?'

'Oh, yes.' She laughed nervously again. 'Aidan's an extremely nice person and I shouldn't have . . . will you just forget I said anything?' Her pale eyes stared anxiously at me.

'Yes, of course,' I replied. 'Consider it wiped from my memory bank.'

'Thanks Chloe.' Then she dug into her pocket and produced a large bar of fruit and nut chocolate. 'I bought this today but I can't eat any more. So it's spare,' she said.

'Oh,' I said, thinking she was going to offer it to me.

'I thought Aidan might like it,' she went on. 'Would you give it to him for me, please?'

'Yes, of course.'

'And make sure you say it's from me.'

I wandered into the classroom. Aidan

was crouched over his drawing. He didn't even notice me come in, he seemed to be lost in that picture.

'Hi,' I said. 'Alison's got a spare bar of chocolate and thought you might like it.'

He looked up for a second. 'Fruit and nut, my favourite,' he muttered. Then without another word he returned to his drawing.

Later, Alison hissed at me. 'Did you give Aidan the chocolate?'

'I certainly did. He said it was his favourite.'

'And did you say it was from me?'

'Oh, yes.'

A look of relief shot across Alison's face. Then she scampered off like a frightened rabbit.

Chapter Four

That night Aidan came round my house
again. He had a present for Harvey: an
enormous chew. Harvey pounced on it at
once.

'He'll be your friend for life now,' I said.

'I've got something for you too,' said
Aidan. 'But you don't have to keep it.'
From the pad under his arm Aidan
produced a sketch of Harvey's head and
neck.

'It's excellent,' I cried. And it was.
'When did you do this?'

'After I left you I sat up in my attic for
a while and did it then.'

'It's a really good likeness.'

'The secret is getting the shape of the

head right,' said Aidan. 'That's what takes the longest.'

'Well, I'll definitely pin it up. It'll brighten up my bedroom too. Can I have a look at your other drawings?'

'If you want.'

There were several really good pictures of tigers, elephants and monkeys.

'I did those after I'd been to the zoo. They inspired me.'

Then there was a drawing of a large book, but Aidan had given it legs too. The next was of a tree but with a monkey's face peering out of it.

'That's a monkey tree,' he said. Then he grinned. 'Practically everything I draw turns into some kind of animal in the end.'

I looked at him. 'You're so different from how you are at school.'

'How do you mean?'

'You're all friendly and relaxed here but in class – well, I've seen corpses with more sparkle. You never ever smile.'

'You've got to keep your guard up at school,' said Aidan. 'You can't be yourself there.'

'But they act towards you as if you're a prince or something. And does Alison often give you bars of chocolate?'

'Let's not talk about them.' Then he leant forward and pretended to be listening to Harvey. 'What's that, Harvey? All right, I'll tell her.' He looked up. 'Harvey says can we go for a walk please?'

'What, now?'

'That's what Harvey said.'

'Bit cold, isn't it?'

'We can wrap up. And there's so much to see now.'

'In October!'

'Yeah, this is a brilliant time. It's when the trees really start to show off: they're turning amazing colours out there.' He turned to Harvey. 'Walkies!'

Harvey immediately dropped the chew and came over to me, his tail wagging furiously. Then he began prodding me with his cold, wet nose.

'Looks like you're out-voted,' laughed Aidan.

So we set off in coats and with a torch

35

which Mum insisted we take with us. 'Can I ... would you mind if I held Harvey?' asked Aidan.

'No, of course not.' I handed the lead to Aidan. His face lit up.

'You haven't got a dog of your own then?' I asked.

'No, my mum is allergic to them, so it's just not possible.'

'That's a shame. You'll have to share Harvey with me instead.'

We walked out of my road and then Aidan said, 'There's a wood just down there.'

'Where?'

He pointed. 'Follow me.'

Half-running we came to this turning. 'This leads into it,' said Aidan. 'Come on, it's great there.'

The dead leaves crunched and crackled under our feet. Trees crowded above us, their branches like huge, dark arms. A bird flew far above our heads with a warning cry.

And then we heard a new sound.

Footsteps.

Someone was pounding towards us. Harvey started to bark. I shone my torch ahead of me.

'It's probably just someone out jogging,'

said Aidan. But I sensed he wasn't as calm as he sounded.

The footsteps drew nearer.

Then I let out a whistle of surprise. 'It's Tom from our class,' I said. 'Whatever can he want?'

Aidan didn't answer.

Tom sprinted up to us so out of breath he couldn't speak at first. And the only sound was Harvey barking. Finally he said to Aidan, 'I've been trying to find you . . . You've got to help me.'

Aidan shot Tom a glance as if to warn him not to say anything in front of me.

Tom hesitated. 'I need to tell you something.'

'Not now,' snapped Aidan.

'Yes, it has to be now and only you can . . .' His voice fell to a frightened whisper. 'Tonight they came back.'

'Who came back?' I asked.

'It's nothing,' murmured Aidan, handing me Harvey's lead. 'You go on ahead, Chloe. I'll catch you up in a second.'

I hated being locked out of the conversation like that. And I trudged away very slowly letting Harvey sniff everything he wanted. But neither Tom nor Aidan began talking until I was out of earshot.

I took a sneaky look back at them. Tom was waving his hands about. He seemed very agitated. While Aidan was standing completely still – the way teachers do when they're hearing why you haven't done your homework.

I desperately wanted to know what they were saying.

At long last Aidan came chugging over to me. 'What was all that about?' I asked.

'Nothing much.' He looked away from me. He was lying.

'Tom was really upset,' I continued.

Aidan just shrugged his shoulders. 'He thought I could help him.'

'Why you?'

He looked at me. 'Do you really want to know?'

'Yes.' I practically shouted at him. He hesitated.

'Come on, please tell me.'

'OK.' He frowned. 'If you must know I hold the world record for something.'

'You do?'

He sighed as if it was a big responsibility. 'Yes I do.'

I was very intrigued now. 'But that's great. So tell me all about it.'

He lowered his voice. 'I hold the world record for eating pickled onions.'

'What!'

'It's true. I can eat a whole bathful in just seven minutes. My parents timed me. Actually, my bath is full of pickled onions now, ready for . . .' He couldn't say any more because I was punching him.

'Pickled onions. That's the stupidest thing I've ever heard,' I cried.

Aidan started laughing. Then he grabbed Harvey and ran off.

'Come back here, Onion Breath,' I yelled.

We raced all the way back to my house. 'I'm never going to believe anything you tell me again,' I cried.

Aidan's grin stretched from ear to ear.

But later when I was on my own I realized he had cleverly managed to avoid answering any of my questions. I thought again of how scared Tom had looked tonight.

There was a mystery here.

Somehow, Aidan was right in the middle of it.

And I was just longing to find out what it was.

Chapter Five

Some days later Aidan brought some maths notes round for me. They were incredibly useful. I was having a go at some of the problems when Harvey started scratching at the door. He's a good dog and always lets you know when he needs to go out to the garden.

Aidan took him out while I finished this one last maths problem. Then I spotted Aidan's sketch pad. He'd mentioned that he'd done another drawing of Harvey: a full-length one this time. I thought I'd take a peek.

I rifled through the drawings of lions and elephants which I'd seen before. And then tucked away at the back of the pad I spied another picture. This one was folded in half. On the back of the picture were two words which jumped right out at me.

THE FRIGHTENERS.

They were in deep red capitals. So what was on the other side? A picture of the Frighteners? I was quite intrigued.

I was about to unfold the picture when Aidan burst in, gave this tiger-spring and snatched it out of my hands. It all happened in an instant. I gaped at him, blinking with shock.

He glowered over me. 'What on earth are you doing?'

'I was just . . . I was looking for the new picture of Harvey, that's all.'

'Well, you had no business going through my things!' He stood there, bursting with anger.

'I'm truly sorry. I didn't realize it was private.'

He started to calm down. He put the picture back into his pad. Then he noticed Harvey, who was cowering by the door. He looked at me.

'Whenever anyone shouts, Harvey thinks they're telling him off,' I said.

He immediately knelt down and gave Harvey a big hug. His hands were still trembling, though.

Later I said to him, 'Now, don't get mad again but why didn't you want me to see that picture?'

'Because it's not finished yet ... and I hate it when people look at my stuff before it's ready.'

'Well, it sounds really interesting. Who exactly are the Frighteners?'

'Oh, just forget about it,' he said. 'I may not even finish it.' He pulled out another picture from his pad. 'Here's the new one of Harvey.'

I took it from him. 'It's excellent. And so detailed too. It must have taken you ages.'

'It's yours,' he said. 'I did it for you.' He'd taken enormous care over this drawing. It was a brilliant present. And yet I kept thinking of that other picture, the one Aidan didn't want me to see. Why had he got so worked-up about it?

Shortly afterwards, Aidan got up. 'I'm not feeling so good.'

'What's the matter?'

'I've had this headache all day. Now it's getting worse. I'd better go.'

Aidan gave Harvey a pat, slipped the pad under his arm and left. But those two words hung around my room like a stale perfume.

THE FRIGHTENERS.

Aidan had lied to me. Those words did mean something. And if I'd been able to see the picture I'd have known who, or what they were.

THE FRIGHTENERS.

They stood for something bad, didn't they? My heart thudded.

I'd question Aidan some more tomorrow.

I had to know.

Chapter Six

But next day Aidan was away from school. I was surprised at how much I missed him.

Mr Karr was really stressed out that morning. So when he told us to write our long stories out in silence no-one disobeyed him. The room was totally quiet, except for the scratching of pens.

Then I glanced up and saw my pencil case had gone from my desk. It had been there the last time I looked but now it seemed to have vanished. I checked under my desk but I wasn't really expecting to see it there.

Someone sniggered. I looked round. 'Who's got my pencil case?' I whispered.

No-one seemed to hear me. It was as if I'd vanished too.

Then Tanya turned round and smirked at me.

'Where's my pencil case?' I demanded.

'How should I know,' she replied.

Of course she knew all right. 'You're just too pathetic,' I cried. 'You all are.'

Mr Karr slammed down the exercise book he was marking. 'Chloe, why are you talking?' he asked, his eyes popping alarmingly. 'You are working in silence. Do you understand?'

'Yes, sir.'

'No-one needs to talk. Is that clear?'

'Yes, sir,' I repeated.

'Well get on with your work and stop disturbing the rest of the class.'

I muttered indignantly to myself but didn't dare say another word until breaktime. Then I went up to Tanya. 'So where's my pencil case then?'

'You mean that fluffy one which is so valuable. I expect you've got it insured, haven't you?' She looked at the girls who were standing near us. They laughed obligingly. 'Your pencil case is where it belongs,' said Tanya.

'What does that mean?' I asked.

'Work it out,' she snapped.

'It's in the bin,' said Tom, standing in the doorway.

'What did you tell her that for?' cried Tanya.

'Because you carry things on too long,' he replied. Then he shook his head and walked out.

I retrieved my pencil case and left too. I told myself I wouldn't let Tanya upset me. She just wasn't worth bothering about.

After break Mr Karr seemed in a slightly better mood. He went over to the blackboard, one of the old-fashioned chalk ones. He pulled the board down and then I froze in horror.

On the blackboard someone had drawn a picture of a broomstick and underneath in massive blue letters: FLY HOME CHLOE, BECAUSE NO-ONE LIKES YOU. I saw Mr Karr staring at the words. I felt my face turning as red as two beetroots. He was going to ask the class who wrote it, wasn't

he? And that would be terrible, because it would make such a big deal out of it.

Suddenly Mr Karr grabbed the rubber and cleaned the board with lightning speed. A big cloud of chalk dust formed all around him. Then he huffed and tutted to himself for a moment. But he never said anything. And I was so grateful to him for that. Still, he had seen it. He knew – if he hadn't known before – how unpopular I was.

I felt humiliated. I sensed everyone in the class was looking at me. I blinked away a stray tear. I wasn't going to let them see how much they'd upset me.

At the end of the lesson I took a deep breath and marched up to Tanya. 'That was a marvellous picture of a broomstick. I had no idea you were so talented.' Then I walked quickly away. I'd never felt so miserable and alone.

I couldn't wait for home-time. The moment I got back I rang Aidan. Less

48

than half an hour later he was round my house sitting in my bedroom, with Harvey on his lap.

'As soon as I'm away they do this,' he murmured. 'And Tanya was so nasty to you. Still, nothing about our class surprises me now.' Then he said, quite gently, 'Chloe, will you forget about this?'

'Yes, I will,' I said firmly.

'I shall put this right.'

'How?'

'I told you once I can look after myself ... well, I can look after you too. You'll see.'

'Is it anything to do with the Frighteners?' I asked.

He started. 'Actually, I'd rather not answer that question. But what I will say is that by this time next week Tanya will be crawling to you, begging your forgiveness.'

'I can't wait for that,' I replied. And I couldn't. 'I wish you'd tell me a bit more about what you're going to do, though.'

He raised his hand. 'Trust me, Chloe, it's better this way.' He got up. 'Now I have work to do if I'm going to set things in motion at school tomorrow.'

'But are you well enough?' I asked. 'You still look very pale.'

'My blood's been drained by a vampire, that's all,' he grinned. 'Anyway, I can't be ill now. I'm on a mission.'

'Well, thanks Aidan,' I began.

'I haven't done anything yet,' he interrupted. 'But just wait. Tanya's about to get the most gruesome surprise of her life.'

Chapter Seven

Next day at breaktime, Aidan disappeared. Usually he stayed in the classroom reading but today he rushed off somewhere. I couldn't follow him because Mr Karr asked me to stay behind for a moment.

He wanted to congratulate me on my maths homework. He said it showed a big improvement and when I went out to the playground I should do a lap of honour to celebrate. I think he was being extra nice to me because of that message on the blackboard.

Then I set off to find Aidan. But he was nowhere to be seen. I hoped he was all right. He'd looked pretty groggy all morning.

In the main playground there was a big crowd around Tanya. We weren't supposed to bring mobile phones into school. But she'd smuggled in her new one to show off to everyone. She said it didn't matter if she lost this one as her mum and dad would easily get her another one.

Then that old bell cranked and everyone streamed back into school. There was a big scramble around the pegs as people picked up their bags. I saw Tanya slip the phone down her coat pocket. It didn't seem a very good hiding place to me, but what did I care.

I was still looking around for Aidan when Tanya let out this terrible cry. Suddenly half the school was surging around her. 'I was just putting my phone away,' she wailed, 'when I found this.'

She held a large piece of paper in her hand. What a fuss about nothing, I thought. Typical of her. But then I noticed how everyone was backing away from Tanya.

'Did you see the picture?' cried a voice.

'No, no, I didn't,' gasped Tanya. 'I just saw the back of it.'

'Well throw it away,' said someone else.

'Go on,' urged other voices.

Finally Tanya closed her eyes and let

the paper flutter out of her hand and on to the ground. I strained forward. And then I made out the writing. Two words in red capitals. THE FRIGHTENERS.

Immediately I knew who had put that picture in Tanya's coat. The only person who was missing at the moment: Aidan.

Tanya stood there shivering until another girl put an arm around her. She led her away. No-one was getting too close to the picture either. No-one, except me.

What was it about those words which created such terror? It must be the drawing on the other side. The one Aidan didn't want me to see.

I crouched down. All around me people were talking about what had happened. I could hear Tanya's voice in the distance exclaiming what a shock she'd had.

So Aidan drew weird pictures called The Frighteners. They must be really eerie if they could make Tanya go hysterical like that.

I bet they wouldn't scare me though.

I reached forward.

'No, Chloe.' All at once Aidan was beside me. I looked up at him.

'Trust me,' he urged. 'Leave it alone, please.'

I hesitated.

But I was burning with curiosity. This was the key to the whole mystery. And one very quick glance couldn't hurt, could it?

I flicked the paper over.

Chapter Eight

I don't think I'll ever forget the strange horror of that picture. It was another of Aidan's animal pictures. Only you wouldn't find this creature in a zoo or anywhere else – except deep at night in a nightmare.

It had a large dog's head with two fangs sticking out of its mouth. But its body was thin and twisty like that of a snake. And half way along its body were black, pointy wings.

There were two of them in the picture. One had its head raised slightly as if it were sniffing the air. And both glared at me through immense, purple eyes, like those of a hate-filled tiger. Only,

55

something was crawling out of the corner of their eyes.

I looked closer and saw, with a shudder of disgust, that it was a white maggot. And then I couldn't bear to look at it any more.

I turned to Aidan. He seemed even paler than before. He shook his head at me, looking sad and angry at the same time. 'Chloe, what have you done?' he began. Suddenly he staggered forward. At the same time Mr Karr rushed over to us.

He sat Aidan down on a chair. Then he put Aidan's head between his knees. I hovered anxiously. 'Go back to the classroom, Chloe,' said Mr Karr. 'I'll look after Aidan now. I think he's caught this nasty bug which has been going round the village.'

I folded the picture up. I'd give it back to Aidan later. I certainly didn't want to keep it. It was too creepy. Still, there was no reason for Tanya to get so hysterical about it.

What could a picture do to you?

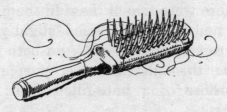

Aidan never came back to the classroom that day. He was sent home. But the pupils in my class kept watching me, their eyes popping out on stalks.

At the end of the day I went up to Alison. 'I get the feeling everyone's studying me today. Am I right?'

She didn't answer at first, just laughed nervously. Then she asked, 'Have you still got the picture?'

'Yes, it's here in my bag.'

At once she moved away from me. 'And did you look at it?' Her voice was hardly a whisper now.

'Yes I did. And I . . .' I stopped. Alison's eyes had widened with alarm.

'Why . . . what's wrong? Afraid it will give me nightmares?'

She tried to smile but couldn't. 'Just be sure and tell Aidan what you've done.'

'But he knows, he was there.'

'Oh, well you're safe then.'

Now my skin was starting to go cold. 'What do you mean safe?'

She hesitated.

'Alison, please tell me. Safe from what?'

'From the Frighteners of course,' she whispered. 'But Aidan's your friend. He wouldn't set them on you.'

'Set them on me!' I practically shrieked.

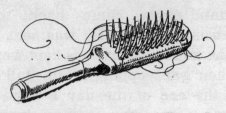

'Whatever do you mean?'

Alison was looking really anxious now. 'I don't mean anything. Honestly. Look, Aidan's the one to ask. I must go, my mum's waiting. Bye.'

The second I got home I rang Aidan. His mother answered. She was really friendly. She said Aidan was feeling much better. But he was asleep right now.

'Will you tell him I called,' I said. 'And ask him to ring me as soon as he can.'

'Of course I will, dear,' replied his mum. 'And thank you very much for calling.'

But Aidan didn't ring me that evening. Maybe he felt groggy again and couldn't get to the phone. Maybe.

I took his picture out of my bag. I stared and stared at it. I'd liked all his other pictures but not this one.

And then I started back in horror. One of those creatures had just moved. The one with its head in the air. It turned and leered right back at me. My heart thundered.

I gazed at the picture again. Nothing moved now. And then I began to relax. I even managed to smile. I knew exactly what had happened.

If you stare at any picture long enough the figures on it seem to move, don't they? It's just a trick of the eyes. I still turned the picture over though, and buried it under my bed.

My bedroom's scary enough at night. It's all to do with not having a carpet yet. Just bare floorboards. And don't they creak. I never notice them during the day. But at night they're always waking me. I jump up, certain a burglar is tip-toeing round my room (though what he'd find to steal I don't know).

But that night a new sound woke me up. A kind of hissing noise, but not hissing like a flat tyre. This was a really angry sound, the kind cats make when they're about to have a fight with someone, like a battle-cry. I thought a cat must be outside warning someone off its territory. But it had sounded so loud, just as if the cat was in my bedroom, hissing and spitting at me.

Now I was being really, really stupid. But I still had to switch the light on just to be sure. Nothing stirred. My room was empty of everything spooky, including mad cats. Finally, I drifted off to sleep again.

The next day was Saturday and I enjoyed not having to rush off to school. Instead, I got up leisurely. And then the silliest thing happened. I couldn't find my hairbrush. I searched everywhere. I was sure I'd left it on my little dressing table last night.

Finally Mum appeared, holding my brush.

'Oh great, where did you find it?'

'On the kitchen table.'

I started. 'How on earth did it get there?'

'Well it didn't fly there,' smiled Mum. 'I don't know who's worse – you or your dad – for leaving your things lying about.'

Now Mum was right, I am incredibly messy and untidy. But still, why would I have left it in the kitchen? I never brush my hair there.

Yet, I must have taken it downstairs. How else could it have got there?

Chapter Nine

That morning the rain hammered furiously against the window while I waited for Aidan to call.

The phone kept ringing. First off it was my Auntie Gwen ringing up for a gossip. She was on the line for ages. Then it was someone for my dad: I don't even remember who now. And then, at last, a call for me: Kara. It was great hearing all the gossip from my old school. But what had happened to Aidan?

The morning crawled past and he never rang. That was so mean of him. He was having a sulk, wasn't he? He must be very cross. I know he begged me not to turn that picture over. And I really wish I hadn't now. It was a truly horrible picture and he could have it back whenever he wanted. But I didn't understand what he was getting in such a state about. It was only a picture after all. I kept saying that to myself.

Late in the afternoon it finally stopped raining. Although black clouds still swarmed menacingly across the sky.

'There'll be another downpour soon,' warned Mum.

But I had to get out for a bit. So I took Harvey for a walk, promising Mum I wouldn't go very far.

Harvey and I came to that turning for the wood which Aidan had shown us. Harvey looked up at me, wagging his tail enthusiastically.

'All right then,' I said.

So we scrunched along with this amazing roof of leaves above our heads. It made the wood dark and mysterious. But it also seemed strangely empty today. No birds fluttered about, no leaves stirred.

Everything was deadly quiet.

'Harvey, I think everyone's gone off for their winter holidays,' I said. 'We've got this wood to ourselves.'

But we weren't completely alone. For then I saw a branch start to bob up and down. And there was a squirrel clinging on to it like Spiderman.

I'd never seen a squirrel close up before. In fact, in London I hadn't seen many animals at all except for dogs and cats and the odd hamster. So I was quite fascinated by it. Then Harvey noticed him and gave a low, warning growl. At once the squirrel did a little bounce, then scurried off up the tree.

'Harvey, you are a nuisance. You've scared him away.'

I looked around me. A grey dusk was settling over the wood. 'We must go back,' I murmured to Harvey.

Ahead of me I could make out the odd shape of a tree or a branch. But otherwise, there was just this dark emptiness. Then, out of the corner of my eye I saw a flash of movement. It was some way ahead of us. A black shape about the size of a fox, maybe a bit smaller.

'Don't scare this animal away too,' I

said to Harvey. Was it a baby fox or a badger? I wasn't sure. But then I'm hopeless on nature. Aidan would have known. I strained forward. It wasn't making any noise. It just stood there, watching Harvey and me.

'Come a bit nearer so I can see what you are,' I whispered. 'Don't be afraid of us.'

It didn't budge. I wasn't really surprised. This was obviously an animal who lived deep in the wood and wasn't used to humans blundering about. In the end I decided to let it stay private and set off back home.

We'd gone a little way when I turned round, expecting the animal to have gone by now. But it was still there. And actually, it was about the same distance away from us as before. For the first time I became – well, not scared exactly – but a bit unnerved.

'Are you following us?' I called.

Harvey began to growl.

But the animal didn't seem the least bit alarmed. It just stayed very still. And it merged so well into the background it was hard to see it at all. But I knew it was there.

Then, all at once I glimpsed something which made me freeze with shock. I saw its eyes. They glowed. And they were purple. I was too stunned to do anything but gape at it.

The next moment something shot past my legs. I caught my breath in terror. What was that? Then I heard Harvey barking and yelping at me. He'd slipped his lead and was telling me to follow him.

'I'm right behind you, Harvey,' I murmured. I dived after him. Branches kept brushing against my face. It was as if they were trying to stop me leaving. And then I must have tripped over a root or something because I just went flying on to the ground. I lay there covered in wet slimy mud and dead leaves. 'I hate the country,' I spluttered.

It had suddenly got very cold too. A really deep chill surrounded me. Then, from out of the air came a sound which stopped me in my tracks. It was that strange, hissing noise I'd heard last night.

Only if anything, it sounded angrier now.

If I looked around, would I see that creature with the glowing purple eyes? I was sure I would. That's why I didn't dare to turn round.

Ahead of me Harvey was barking loudly, urgently. He was urging me on. I just had to get out of here. Somehow I stumbled to my feet. I was shaking all over, but luckily nothing seemed to be broken.

So then I ran for my life. I seemed to be running for ages too. I didn't hear the creature again but I sensed he was still close by, still trailing me. I can't tell you how relieved I was to finally scramble out onto the pathway. Harvey started hurling himself onto me, trying to jump up and lick my face.

'You saw it too, didn't you?' I said to Harvey. I turned around but there was nothing behind us. It had gone – for now.

At home Mum saw me and had twenty fits. 'Look at you!' she exclaimed. 'You'll have to take all those clothes off right away.'

Later I sat drying my hair, with Harvey asleep on my bed and rain streaming down my window. But in my mind I was back in the wood, seeing again that hideous creature with the purple eyes.

And I knew I hadn't seen a real animal. I'd seen a supernatural one.

Chapter Ten

Aidan's picture had put a spell on me.

I was having my tea when that idea came to me. After I'd stopped choking I ran through all the strange things which had happened since I'd taken the picture: hissing noises in my bedroom at night; hairbrushes which strolled downstairs and that shadowy figure stalking us in the wood – its eyes the same as the ones in Aidan's picture.

It couldn't just be a coincidence, could it?

'Are you all right?' Mum smiled across the table at me.

Then Dad scrutinised me. 'Your mother's cooking is not that bad, is it?'

I smiled faintly but I couldn't eat any more. I could hardly even swallow. My head was whirling. I'd been put under a spell. But how long for? And what else was going to happen to me? I had to talk to Aidan.

As soon as I could I escaped to the phone and dialled Aidan's number really quickly. No answer. I couldn't believe it. I tried again a few minutes later. Still no reply.

I sat staring at the television. What could I do now? The question chased around and around in my head. But what was the answer? Then Dad came in and switched the television down. 'Now, what's up?' he asked.

I shrugged. 'Nothing.'

'Oh, that's all right then.' But he sat down and went on looking at me.

Finally I burst out. 'Dad, do you believe that pictures – nasty pictures – can put spells on people?'

'Why? You're not going to put a spell on me, are you?'

I grinned. 'Not sure yet. No, it's just I've been reading this really nutty story. It's about a boy who gives someone a spooky picture and then spooky things start happening to that person.'

Dad shook his head. 'Remind me not to read it.'

'But in real life, can people put a spell on you?'

'Yes.' Dad smiled at the look of amazement on my face. 'Want me to tell you how the spell works?'

I nodded.

Dad thought for a moment. 'Well, it's quite simple. You plant an idea in someone's mind really strongly. And then their mind makes it come true. Take those old witch doctors. Now they were always putting spells on someone. They'd say, at eleven o'clock next Wednesday you're going to see a little green monster and at eleven o'clock on Wednesday . . .'

'They'd see a little green man,' I interrupted.

'Exactly. The witch doctor had made them believe it would happen, and it did.'

'And could they make someone hear

things too – like hissing noises, for example?'

'Very easily. Our imagination is a wonderful, amazing gift but you've got to be careful with it. If you let it overpower you, you can scare yourself half to death. But no-one can really put a spell on anyone else. That's . . .' He paused.

'A load of old goose droppings,' I prompted.

'Well, I don't know if that's exactly the phrase I would have used. But yes, that's the idea. And I'd read another book tonight if I were you.'

That night I said over and over to myself: all the spooky things which have happened are just in my imagination. No-one can really put a spell on you. I fell asleep still chanting that.

In the morning I woke up and stretched. I hadn't had any nightmares. I looked at my dressing table. There was my hairbrush just as I'd left it. Nothing else was missing either.

Dad was right, I'd just been imagining things. Like that creature I saw in the woods. It could have been anything. Especially as I don't know much about woodland animals. And was I totally certain it had purple eyes?

I felt much better when I went downstairs. Then Dad announced he'd planned a treat for today: we were going to the cinema this afternoon. When we lived in London I saw a new film practically every week. It was the only way we could pull Dad away from his work, as he loves films.

We drove to the station, then took the train into town. It took ages, stopping at stations with long, unpronounceable names. Then we had a meal out. Dad doesn't approve of eating in the cinema, not even popcorn.

At the cinema, though, the family in front of us had a different idea. They lay back with their feet up, slurping cans of drink and chomping their way through sweets, chocolates and bucket-loads of popcorn.

'It's like sitting in a pig trough,' sniffed Dad. Mum and I both laughed. Then the lights dimmed and the adverts began.

They went on for years. Finally, the film started and I felt a little flutter in my stomach of anticipation. Unfortunately, the girl in the row in front had dropped her popcorn and was scrambling about in the dark for ages. Dad clicked his tongue in irritation.

But then I started to get really involved in the film. It was a comedy about a family of aliens who come to Earth for a holiday. All around me were rumbles of laughter.

I sat back. I was sitting right by the aisle, which is my favourite spot (I hate being in the middle of a row – I feel all closed in). Then I just happened to glance casually into the aisle and noticed someone had brought their dog along. I didn't think that was allowed. I took another look. And then my heart almost stopped. I felt my mouth open in a scream of silent horror.

It was here in the aisle.

Its snake-like body was almost entirely in shadow. All I could really see was a shape that seemed to be floating just above the ground. And its eyes which glowed cat-like in the dark.

Suddenly a burst of light shot across the screen and for a moment I could see the Frightener really clearly. And do you know, it looked exactly like Aidan's picture. It even had that maggot dribbling out of the corner of its eye. It was truly horrible to see. But it was over in a flash.

Then the Frightener was hidden in the shadows again. But I knew it was still there. I could see its body quivering very slightly. And its terrible eyes were staring right at me now.

Suddenly there was this great roar of laughter which made the cinema shake. No-one else had noticed that a monster had crept inside. But they must see it in a moment. You couldn't really miss it. I waited for someone to yell out in terror. But no-one did. They just went on laughing louder and louder. The creature ignored them too. All its hatred was beamed on to me.

'You're not real,' I half-whispered. 'I'm imagining you. When I open my eyes again you'll have vanished.'

I closed my eyes, wishing with all my heart the thing would go away.

I opened them again. But it was still there. Only now I was sure I could hear its wings begin to beat very slowly. And was its body starting to swell up? I thought it was. It was getting ready to attack. Any moment now it would half-glide, half-leap towards me.

'Go away!' I screamed.

'What is it, love?' cried Dad. I was leaning right up against him, shaking and pointing. But I was pointing at the air, the creature had melted away as swiftly as a dream.

An usherette steamed forward, the light from her torch wavering over me. 'Is everything all right?' she asked. She didn't wait for me to answer, just said, 'I'll go and get help,' almost as if she'd been expecting this to happen.

Dad had his arm around me because I was still shaking. And Mum was whispering questions which I couldn't hear properly. There were rustles of conversation all around me and the family in front had even stopped chewing for a moment.

Two more usherettes appeared, armed with torches. One smiled very sadly at me, just as those nurses do on TV when they're about to tell someone they've got seven deadly diseases. She asked if me and my parents would mind coming to the manager's office for a moment. The other one was asking the people in the row in front of us to check all their belongings.

I stumbled up the steps with Mum and Dad either side of me. The usherette escorted us into the office. A surprisingly young man with a pencil-thin moustache was waiting for us.

He asked me to tell him what had happened. I stuttered. But what could I say? That I'd just seen a horrible, winged creature in the aisle which had escaped from a picture. And no-one else could see it because I was under a spell. I'd only make a right show of myself if I said that.

But luckily, I didn't need to say much at all. You see, last night in the cinema someone had spotted a man crawling along empty seats and taking money out of any handbags which were lying on the floor. The thief had escaped. And the manager assured us that was who I'd seen tonight.

So I played along with him. I just said I saw a face. But it was over in a flash. I hardly said anything really. Yet everyone was so kind to me. Then one of the usherettes came in and said that no-one else in the audience had reported anything missing.

The manager looked very relieved. I was relieved too until I remembered the man had not really been here in the first place.

'I think you spotted him before he had time to cause any harm,' said the manager. 'There might even be a small reward for you.'

'Oh no, please don't do that,' I cried. Normally I'd have loved to receive a reward. But not this time. I'd just have felt a total fraud.

So in the end the manager shook me by the hand and gave us some complimentary tickets.

On the train home I was very quiet. Mum and Dad thought I was still in shock. Well I was. I'd so wanted to believe that creature was just down to imagination. But tonight I hadn't given the Frighteners a second thought and still one of them appeared. I couldn't forget those terrible eyes glaring at me. And when it suddenly moved . . . I began to shiver again.

All at once I thought of Aidan. If he could put bad spells on people, I understood why no-one wanted to upset him. Then I remembered something Alison had said to me on my first day. 'Don't get on the wrong side of Aidan.'

Well, I had got on his bad side. But he wasn't just going to leave me to the mercy of these creatures. He was going to take the spell off me, wasn't he?

Before we'd gone out I'd asked Mum to switch the answerphone on. And as soon as we got home I raced over to it, just hoping that at last there'd be a message from Aidan.

But there wasn't. A whole weekend had gone past and he hadn't even bothered to call me. Now I'd never do that to a friend. If someone needed me I'd be there – even if my friend had annoyed me badly.

But Aidan had just abandoned me to the Frighteners. Or that's what it felt like. So now what was I to do?

That night I tossed and turned. I couldn't get off to sleep for ages and ages. Next morning when I looked up daylight was streaming through my curtains. Mum put her head around the door. 'Awake at last.'

'What time is it?' I asked.

'Nearly ten o'clock.'

'What!' I squeaked.

'It's all right. I rang up the school and told them you had a nasty shock yesterday and I'm keeping you home today. Now, how about breakfast in bed?'

'Definitely, bring it on, Mum.' It was nice being fussed over. Then Harvey jumped onto my bed. I was patting him when Mum said, 'By the way, this seems to have a life of its own.'

'What does?'

She waved my hairbrush at me. My skin just went cold.

'Where did you find it?' I asked, in a hoarse whisper.

'Downstairs on the kitchen table again,'

laughed my mum, all bright and breezy.
'I don't know, you and your hairbrush.'
She didn't realize what she was telling
me.

After she'd gone I sank back on the bed.
Even when I was asleep the Frighteners
were close by. They wanted me to know
that too. That's why they'd taken my
hairbrush away.

And they were supernatural creatures,
so there was no way I could stop them.

Only one person could.

Aidan.

Chapter Eleven

I dialled Aidan's number. My hands were sweating already. I knew this was going to be a very awkward conversation.

Part of me felt that Aidan had let me down. After all, it wouldn't have killed him to ring me back, would it. But I needed his help badly. So I was going to have to be nice to him, even crawl a bit.

His mum answered. I asked her how Aidan was.

'Oh, much better, thank you. He'll probably be back at school tomorrow. You called before, didn't you?'

'Yes.'

'Aidan did ring you back?'

'No, he didn't actually,' I said quietly.

'Well I certainly gave him the message, straightaway after you'd rung, in fact. I'll get him for you now.' Then she added, 'I hope you haven't caught Aidan's bug.'

She was probably wondering why I wasn't at school. 'Oh no, I've just been a bit under the weather but I'm fine now, thanks.'

'Oh, good. Well, Aidan won't keep you waiting long.'

But three or four minutes dragged by. What was happening? Then his mum came back on the line. 'I'm so sorry dear, Aidan can't come to the phone right now.'

I felt a wrenching in my stomach. Aidan really had turned his back on me. 'Oh well,' I said faintly, 'thanks for trying anyway.'

'I will ask him to call you,' repeated Aidan's mum.

'Thanks,' I murmured. But I knew there wasn't any chance of that.

Then she went on. 'I've just had an idea. Why don't you come round for tea this afternoon. We'd love to meet you and you can chat properly with Aidan then.'

I jumped at the chance to meet Aidan face to face. So it was quickly arranged. I would go round to his house at four o'clock today.

As soon as I got off the phone I threw the picture of the Frighteners into a bag. I couldn't wait to be rid of it. Even if Aidan refused to talk to me he could still have this back. I never wanted to see it again.

And when I gave the picture back to Aidan the spell would break. Or so I hoped.

His house was the last one in Compass Close.

'Their garden puts ours to shame,' said Mum. And it was a very well looked after garden, still full of colour and with a few late blooming roses round the door.

I said goodbye to Mum, then rang the doorbell. A tiny, grey-haired lady appeared. For a moment I wasn't quite sure if she was Aidan's mum. But then she beamed at me. 'Now, you must be Chloe. Welcome.' She stretched out a hand to me. I'd never shaken hands with a woman before.

'Come in my dear,' she said. She was wearing glasses which made her blue eyes seem even bigger. 'Now, I haven't told Aidan you're coming. I thought it would be a lovely surprise for him.'

Well, it would be a surprise anyway, I thought.

She led me down the hall into a small, very cosy room. There was a log fire crackling away in the corner and just above it, all these brasses glowed cheerfully. Another wall had shelves crammed with books. While on the floor still more books were piled up.

And sitting on the sofa beside the fire was Aidan. He was – surprise, surprise – drawing something in his sketch pad.

'Aidan, I've got a visitor for you.'

I felt my mouth go dry. 'Hi Aidan,' I said, as casually as I could. 'Surprise!'

He looked as if he had never seen me before and didn't want to now.

'Well, I'll leave you for a moment. The food won't be long,' said Aidan's mum. She closed the door.

'I'm glad you're feeling better,' I said.

He just gave me this really withering glare.

I swallowed hard. Despite the warm fire, the air was full of icicles.

I burrowed in my bag and brought out the picture of the Frighteners. 'This is yours.'

Aidan just went on giving me his zombie stare: the one he uses on everyone at school. The silence hung between us like smoke. 'You could at least talk,' I said at last. 'I think it's really pathetic, not even talking.'

And then he did talk. 'Why did you take it?' he demanded, in a voice full of cold fury.

'I don't know. I just wanted to see what the big mystery was all about.'

'But I *told* you not to look at it.'

'I know.'

He shook his head. 'You're just like all the rest, aren't you? Well, give me the picture and go. I'll tell Mum something. I've got nothing more to say to you.'

I slapped the picture down on the coffee table. Then I whirled round on him. 'All right, you asked me not to look at a picture and I did. But you're not my teacher. You don't tell me what to do. And anyway, you'll be pleased to hear I had a really terrible weekend.'

He gave me a sharp look of surprise. 'What do you mean?'

'Where do I start? I've had those vile, nasty creatures turning up all over the place: in my bedroom, when I'm out walking, and would you believe, at the cinema. And even when I'm asleep they're creeping about taking things from my bedroom . . .'

'That's impossible!' he exclaimed.

'Excuse me – I was there.'

'But that was never meant to happen,' he cried, sitting up in horror. 'That picture was meant for Tanya. It was her punishment for being so mean to you. I was helping you.'

'Oh really,' I said, sarcastically.

'Yes. Then you messed everything up by disobeying me. I was cross about that but I'd never set the Frighteners on you.' His voice rose. 'Never!'

'Well anyway, you have,' I cried. 'And how exactly do you take them off me?'

Before Aidan could answer the door opened and his mum bustled in with a tray of biscuits, sandwiches and tea. 'Why are you still standing up, Chloe? Honestly, Aidan, what kind of host are you? You sit beside Aidan on the sofa dear. Now, that's much better, isn't it.'

The tray clanged down on the coffee table, completely covering Aidan's picture of the Frighteners.

Aidan's mum handed me a plate. 'Take a chocolate biscuit before Aidan scoffs them all,' she laughed. 'He's very partial to chocolate, which explains why he's got to have three fillings at the dentist's after school tomorrow.'

'Don't remind me,' groaned Aidan.

'Well, just to save Aidan's teeth I will have one,' I said, taking a chocolate biscuit.

'Now tuck in dear,' said Aidan's mum.

'Because we're very informal here,' boomed a voice from the doorway.

A man rolled in swaying from side to side. I gaped at him in alarm. Was he drunk? Then Aidan whispered. 'My dad's got arthritic knees,' and immediately I blushed, feeling as if Aidan had read my mind.

'Chloe, delighted to meet you,' he said. Then, wheezing a bit, he eased himself into a chair. He had wispy, grey hair and a very lined face. But he was smartly dressed in a tweed jacket and dark blue shirt. He was very friendly too.

He told me he was a writer. He wrote books about famous British films of the past. He showed me one of his books, 'A WARTIME SCREEN. BRITISH CINEMA 1939— 1945.'

'It must be just brilliant to see your name on the front of a book,' I said. He and his wife laughed in a pleased sort of way. 'I bet my dad would like to read this book. He loves films.'

'We've turned our garage into a projection room,' he went on. 'Our own private cinema we call it. We'll watch a film made fifty or more years ago, Aidan too – and as soon as the film starts the years just fall away. We're spellbound once again.'

All the time his dad was talking, Aidan's gaze never left me. It was as if he was watching me to see how I reacted. It was pretty unnerving, actually.

Finally, Aidan's dad got to his feet. 'Back to work,' he said. 'I just want to get my chapter on "The Thief of Baghdad" finished tonight.' Aidan's mum left too, but not before urging us to finish all the cakes and biscuits.

'Your mum and dad are so nice,' I said.

'I expect they're much older than you were expecting,' snapped Aidan.

'A bit, but what does that matter. I really like them.'

Aidan's face softened. 'So do I. Actually, it's because of them that I discovered the Frighteners.'

'What!' I exclaimed. 'You mean they're in on this too.'

'Not exactly, it's just . . .' He suddenly got up. 'We can't talk here. I'll take you up to my attic, if you like.'

'Yes, OK.'

'By the way, I also call it my laboratory.'

'Why?'

'You'll see, it's an amazing place. So come on, follow me.' Then he added, 'And bring the picture too. We'll need that.'

Chapter Twelve

'There's not much light up here so I've brought this,' said Aidan. He held up a lantern. Then he sprinted up some steep, winding steps: obviously he'd done this many times before. I followed a little more slowly.

What did Aidan mean this attic was also his laboratory? My heart was beating louder and louder.

I scrambled inside the attic. It was pretty small, not much bigger than a tree house. And it was high in the middle, but very narrow at the sides. In the middle of the attic were some books, comics, games, and the inevitable sketch pads.

Then on the walls I saw something which made me gasp with horror.

'The Frighteners.' My voice caught on the word. I pointed at the pictures which covered one wall.

'Oh no,' said Aidan. 'They're just ordinary animals.'

But they didn't look very ordinary. There was a bat with large, furry wings. And there was an enormous drawing of a tiger which had exactly the same eyes as those of the Frighteners.

Aidan saw me staring at the tiger. 'Don't worry,' he said. 'It won't suddenly jump down off the wall. Just sit down and make yourself at home.' He gestured me over to the cushions. But Aidan didn't sit down. He hovered over me like an attentive waiter. Above us I could hear the wind whistling.

'We're half out of doors here,' said Aidan. 'So I'm afraid it can get quite draughty. All the noises get magnified too. Sometimes when it's raining really hard you think the roof's about to come off. And you can hear the rain gurgling down all the drainpipes.' He stared down anxiously at me. 'Are you OK?'

'Oh yes, I'm fine,' I murmured, gazing around me. The lantern gave off a quivering, pale light but the corners were full of shadows.

And then I heard something land on the roof with a thud. It made me jump. Aidan laughed. 'It's only a bird, probably a pigeon. They're always landing on the roof. The other day I heard a couple of them having a punch-up. That was incredible.'

'I bet.'

Aidan smiled at me. 'Isn't it great?'

'Yes,' I lied.

'Sometimes when I'm up here the doorbell goes. And it sounds as if the callers are far, far, below me. It's just as if I've climbed to the top of my very own private mountain. No-one ever comes up here except me – and now you.' He sat down opposite me. 'It's because of this attic my whole life has changed.'

'How?' I asked.

'You don't know what I used to be like, do you? Well, last year when we first moved here, I was very shy and introverted. I just sat in the corner all by myself. I'd never say anything to anybody.'

He's exactly the same now, I thought.

'I was new and I didn't fit in. A little bit like you,' he added, with a shy smile. 'Only I hated football and liked reading books and old comics, so I was really odd!

But then I discovered this place, my hideaway. I'd be up here away from everyone, safe in my own world, where I could imagine whatever I wanted.

'Then I made an amazing discovery,' he pointed. 'One of those bricks over there is a browny red colour and a different shape from the others. It intrigued me. So one day I managed to move it. Then I looked behind it and found . . . well, I'll show you.'

He went over to the wall at the end of the attic, moved the brick away, then with a flourish brought out a shell. It was a peachy, orange colour and covered in brown spots which made it look as if it had the measles or something.

I stared down at it. 'And you just found it behind that brick?'

'Yeah. I've no idea who put it there.' He smiled mysteriously. 'A gift from the deep, dark past. Although at the time I had no idea how special this shell was. I just liked it and sometimes I'd put it up to my ear and listen to the sea.'

I smiled. I'd done that.

'Meanwhile at school I'd get picked on sometimes. They'd make jokes about my missing finger. And they'd do stupid things. Like once, they put glue on my chair. Afterwards it looked as if a snail had crawled all over my trousers. I suppose that was quite amusing in a way.

'But then one day they went too far.' His voice began to tremble. 'It was an open evening at our school. There were displays of our work everywhere and we had to talk about what we'd done to our parents. I was in the Art room. I was showing my parents some of my drawings and it was all going great until I heard Tom say in the loudest whisper you've ever heard. "Have you seen Aidan's parents. They're so wrinkly and ancient. They must have had him when they were eighty."'

Then other girls, including Tanya, joined in saying things like, "My grandad's younger than his dad and I thought it was parents evening, not grandparents evening." They just went on and on. But do you know the really awful thing?' His voice tightened. 'My parents never said anything. But I knew by their faces they'd heard every word.'

'Oh, that's terrible,' I said.

Aidan didn't reply at first. He just shook his head as if he was trying to wipe away the scene from his memory.

'When I came home that night I went

straight up here to my hideaway. I was so angry. How dare they be so rude and nasty about my parents? But what could I do to them. Me, the smallest boy in my class with muscles like a sparrow's kneecaps.' He gave a bitter laugh. 'I couldn't do anything to them and they knew it.

'But this anger went on swelling up inside me. Until finally I picked up my shell from behind that brick, still talking furiously to myself. Over and over I wished I could do something, I wished so hard my head hurt. And then the strangest thing happened. I put the shell up to my ear and I didn't hear the sea at all. Instead, I heard a strange kind of hissing noise.'

I started. 'A really angry hissing?'

'That's it,' said Aidan. 'Then I went over to the gap in the wall, where the shell had been and something stared back at me.'

I choked off a cry. 'That's horrible.'

'Not really. It was a shock, of course. But I knew that it was an animal. And no animal scares me. I just stood watching until it flew out of the tunnel and quickly formed into the strangest creature you've ever seen. A bit of everything really, with a dog's head and a snake's body, a bat's wings . . .'

'I know. We've met,' I murmured.

Aidan continued. 'I was a bit alarmed by it at first. It half-flew around the attic and stood looking at me for awhile. Then it just faded into the darkness and was gone.'

'Did it come back again?' I asked.

'Not at first. I even wondered if it had all been a dream. I have fallen asleep up here sometimes.'

I shivered. I didn't think I could ever sleep up here.

'But I didn't want to forget the animal I'd seen. So I drew a picture of him. I suppose drawing's a kind of magic, isn't it: a way of bringing someone back to life.

And I wanted to see that creature again so badly.'

I stared at him in amazement. 'But why? It's like the worst, most yukky bits of every animal all put together. It's even got a maggot popping out of its eye.'

'And you don't like that?'

'No, it's disgusting.'

'Do you really think so?' Aidan sounded a bit surprised. 'Well, it fascinated me and I knew it was on my side.'

'How did you know that?'

'I don't know. I just did. Anyway, one night I discovered how to bring it back. I had the shell and was whispering, "I wish you'd come back. Please come back." But nothing happened. So then I closed my eyes. I thought I could concentrate better with my eyes shut and wished very hard that I could conjure up those creatures again. And then it happened. I saw this wisp of smoke. The next moment it came floating out of the gap in the wall again.'

'So just by talking into the shell . . .'

'That's right. They hear me through the shell. It's like my control centre.'

'They?'

He nodded. 'At first just the one came. But then as it got to know me . . .'

'It brought its mates,' I interrupted.

Aidan smiled. 'That's right. There are seven of them now.'

'Get a few more and you can start your own football team. And do you call them up every night?'

'Oh yes. They like me to talk to them. I'm their friend and trainer. I like to draw them too. The Frighteners, as I call them. But at first I thought only I could see them.'

'How wrong you were. So when did you find that out?'

'One lunchtime I was in the art room doing a painting of the Frighteners. I'd spent ages on it. I was really proud of it. Then this boy – who wasn't even in my class – just came and snatched it away.

'He said he'd give it back to me if I gave him ten pounds. Well, I didn't have ten pounds. And I knew that my parents couldn't . . . money's a bit tight just now. But the boy refused to take anything less and said he'd tear up the picture if I didn't get him the cash.

'That got me very angry, so in a kind of wild desperation I said, "I'm warning you. Tear up that picture and the Frighteners will haunt you for the rest of your life."

'He laughed.

'So I shouted, "All right, I'm setting the Frighteners on you right now." But he just said, "You're crazy," and repeated his threat.'

Well, I tried hard to earn extra cash. I did these jobs for the neighbours. But I was also so frustrated. Why should I have to pay that boy money? And at night I would talk to the Frighteners, just like you talk to Harvey. I'd whisper into the shell, "I wish you really could follow my picture and terrify that boy who took it." I even told them how to scare him. In my head I imagined all kinds of spooky things. But I never expected anything to happen.' He paused for a moment, seeing how intently I was listening. 'Then, Chloe, came a great moment in my life.

'At school one morning, that boy was waiting for me. He looked terrible. "What have you done to me?" he cried. "Those creatures are terrorizing me! They're everywhere. I can't get to sleep. Take the spell off me, please."'

Aidan leaned forward, a new brightness in his eyes. 'The creatures had done what I'd asked. All that day stars were exploding inside my head. I'd discovered something truly astonishing. I could protect myself through – well I call it – magic thinking.'

'And what exactly is that?' I asked.

'It means that if I think about something very hard – really picture it inside my head – I can make it real. Now, is that skill or what?' He smiled triumphantly at me.

'Dr Frankenstein has got nothing on you, has he?'

Aidan grinned. 'That's right, because he had to mess about with machines to bring his monster to life. I just need this,'

he tapped his head, 'and the shell, of course. So don't worry, Chloe,' he went on, 'you need never fear anyone again. Not with me as your friend. And just remember, I'm not the smallest boy in my class any more. Now I'm more powerful than any of them.'

He looked so happy I thought he was going to start dancing a jig or something.

'It was such a great feeling,' he continued, 'knowing I could put a spell on anyone I wanted. Kings, prime ministers, anyone. Soon I made up a list. Right at the top was Tom. I had to pay him back for what he'd said about my mum and dad.

'I drew another picture of the Frighteners – just a sketch this time – then I whispered into my shell, "Whoever sees this picture first, follow that person home tonight and haunt them."

'Next day when Tom wasn't looking I slipped the picture into his bag. He didn't discover it until he got home. What a shock that must have given him.

'The following evening Tom was playing football with some of his mates. The ball went hurtling into the bushes. Tom went to get it and saw one of the Frighteners.'

'It was in the bushes . . .?'

'That's right. Tom went deathly pale and couldn't play football any more that evening. He just ran off home. But on the way he thought he saw the Frighteners again. This time he tripped and fell. He sprained his ankle, couldn't play football again for weeks. And the incredible thing is, I hadn't trained the Frighteners to do these extra hauntings. They were doing them spontaneously.'

All of a sudden I remembered something. 'That night in the wood when Tom came running after us . . .' I began.

'Now that was really silly,' interrupted Aidan. 'I'd taken the spell off Tom by then. But he's saying the Frighteners are still haunting him. He keeps on at me to make them go away, but actually, they've gone already. He just won't believe me.'

I wondered how Aidan could be so certain. But then I thought, the Frighteners are under his control. So if Aidan said they've gone, then they must have. Perhaps Tom had been frightened so badly he was starting to imagine them now. I couldn't help feeling a bit sorry for him.

'Next on my list was Helen. She was only at our school for a while, thank goodness. But she was a right stirrer and she was very nasty about my mum and dad. So I sent her a picture. And she even saw the Frighteners during the day. She said she saw them looking through the window at her when she was at school. And the sun shone right through them. Well, it's possible, I suppose. My Frighteners are very clever. Of course the whole school knows about them now.'

'That's why everyone practically kisses your feet.'

'No, some people just avoid me, in fact, they run if I even glance in their direction. But that's cool too. By the way, I've never asked for any presents, but a few do give me the odd bar of chocolate.'

'Like poor Alison.'

'But I know they're only nice to me because they're scared of me. And I didn't want it to be like that with you.' His eyes met mine for a moment. 'I wanted us to be proper friends. That's why I told the class not to breathe a word to you. But actually

103

I'm glad you know now. It's good sharing it with someone.'

A slow smile spread across his face. 'And isn't it the most astounding, incredible thing you've ever heard?'

'I can truthfully say it is. But Aidan, I still don't know . . . what exactly are the Frighteners?'

He shrugged his shoulders. 'I'm not sure. Somehow I just conjured them up—' He waved his hand around. 'And I can call them up whenever I want, with the help of my shell, of course.'

'But they're not ghosts, are they?'

'Not exactly – although they can appear and disappear like ghosts. Like I said, I just wished hard for them and there they were.' He grinned. 'It's a magic place, this attic.'

I gazed around. Magic wasn't the word I'd have used. The darkness was thickening. Everything in this room seemed to be fading except for those creatures on the walls.

Was it my imagination or were they growing bigger? I gazed at that tiger. Its eyes glowed in the darkness, just like the Frighteners.

I began to tremble.

'Will you tell that tiger to stop staring at me?'

Aidan laughed. He thought I was joking.

I glanced around me. The attic was full of shadows now.

And then one of the shadows moved.

My trembling quickened.

And I waited for it to slowly creep out of the darkness.

Chapter Thirteen

'Aidan,' my voice began to crack. 'I think I saw something.' I pointed.

He barely even turned round. 'Yes, one of the Frighteners is here.'

I drew my breath in sharply. 'But I thought they only appeared when you summoned them up on the shell.'

'At first that was true, but once I've moved the brick away I let them come and go as they want.'

I gazed anxiously into the dimness. 'I can't see it at all now.'

'That's because I've taught the Frighteners to sneak and hide. They're more unsettling like that. But haven't you noticed how chilly it's suddenly got?'

'Well, yes, I suppose I have,' I said.

'That's a sure sign the Frighteners are here. They always bring icy air with them. Now look again, you'll see it, if you're patient.'

'I don't know if I want to,' I replied. But I found myself peering really hard into that gloomy corner. I could see a massive cobweb glinting faintly in the dim light. But nothing else.

All at once I heard something. Was it just the wind whining away to itself? Or could it be . . . yes, it must be, as Aidan was getting really worked-up.

'Chloe, you must see it now. You must. Look! Look.'

I squinted up my eyes and then I could make out something edging slowly forward, half crouching in the shadows.

'Yes I see it,' I gasped. 'I do.'

'About time,' replied Aidan. 'Just look at those wings perched on the middle of its body. Aren't they great?'

'They look like a tiny, black tent, don't they?'

'That's it exactly,' said Aidan.

Then I heard that hissing noise again. 'I don't think it's exactly overjoyed to see me,' I whispered. 'And now I can't see it again. Why does it keep melting away?'

'Because it can,' replied Aidan. 'A Frightener is able to slip off in the blink of an eye and reappear just as quickly. But don't be afraid of them.'

'Oh, of course not,' I laughed.

'No, honestly. Anyway, I think it's time I took the spell off you.'

'Strangely enough, so do I.'

He picked up the shell and began talking into it as if it were a mobile phone. His voice was very low and gentle. He could have been talking to a nervous dog.

'You have done extremely well. But do not follow the picture any more. I command you to come home. Come home.' He repeated this several times. Then he tore up the picture.

'Only I can tear it up,' he said. 'No-one else.' Then he leaned forward. 'Chloe, you are now released from the spell.'

'About time,' I exclaimed. Then I let out a gasp. I was convinced I could see another Frightener, floating out of the

darkness. It was skimming just above the ground, its wings beating very slowly. It brought a cold breeze into the attic.

'Don't be frightened of them,' said Aidan. Suddenly he placed the shell in my hand. 'The ones who are far away try and talk to me.'

'Those funny hissing sounds?'

'Yes, go on, listen.'

My hand shook as I put the shell to my ear but all I could hear was the sea. 'Sorry, they're not coming through.'

He took the shell back and listened. 'But I can hear them all right. Try again.'

But again they didn't come through for me.

'How very strange,' said Aidan. 'I think you are just too scared of them. Try again and . . .'

'Not right now, thanks,' I interrupted.

And then I heard something like a rustling noise. I looked up in alarm. 'Now, what's that?'

'It's just the wind,' said Aidan. 'It makes the pictures on the walls move.'

I looked up to see that tiger again. Now I was certain its eyes were following me.

'Look, Chloe, just relax,' urged Aidan. 'Remember, everything in this room is under my control.'

Suddenly I thought of something. 'Did you teach the Frighteners to take things from people's rooms at night?'

Aidan clapped his hands in delight. 'No, I just taught them the basics of scaring people. They must have improvised that one. It can't be easy for them either, moving objects. But they're so clever, aren't they . . . and so keen. I don't know what they'll do tomorrow night when they visit Tanya.'

'Tanya!' I exclaimed.

'She was very spiteful to you. She's still got to be punished,' continued Aidan. 'And she will. Tomorrow she will receive the picture, just as I'd planned before. I need your help, by the way. I want you to distract Tanya's attention at breaktime while I'm delivering her picture.'

I'm no friend of Tanya's. But I was still shocked that Aidan was giving her another picture. I opened my mouth to say something, but then closed it again. I didn't think Aidan would understand. And I suppose she deserved it.

There were shadows on Aidan's face now. In fact, I could hardly see him. The Frighteners were hard to make out too. A couple of times I'd see a flicker of movement out of the corner of my eye.

That was all. But I sensed them circling around me like sharks.

All at once I couldn't stay here another second. I jumped up, banging my head on the low ceiling.

'Are you all right?' asked Aidan.

'Yes, fine,' I replied. 'It's just, I said I'd be home ages ago so I'd better go.'

'Well, I'll walk you back.'

'There's no need,' I whispered.

'Of course I will.'

We clambered down the winding steps. 'So now you know where I really live,' said Aidan.

'Yes,' I murmured. 'Spooky place, isn't it?'

'Not when you get used to it,' he said quickly. We stood in the hall. 'My mum and dad must be in the garage watching another film.'

'Well, don't disturb them, say goodbye from me and thanks for . . .'

A loud cracking noise like a twig

snapping made us both jump. Someone had slipped a letter through the box.

'The postman's a bit late today,' I said. Then we heard footsteps running away. Aidan's face tightened. He went over, snatched up the envelope and tore it open. There was a card inside. He stared at it trembling. Without a word he handed it to me. This is what it said: 'AIDAN GRANT IS CASTING BAD SPELLS ON CLASS 6K AND GIVING THEM NIGHTMARES. YOU MUST STOP HIM NOW.' It was written in block capitals and unsigned.

Then I noticed the envelope. It was addressed to Mr and Mrs Grant and marked: 'URGENT'.

'Oh no,' I sighed. 'This is stupid.' Aidan stood there with his head raised in the air. He reminded me of someone. Then with a stab of horror I realized who it was.

The Frighteners put their heads up in the air exactly like that when they're about to attack someone. Aidan's eyes blazed as fiercely as the Frighteners, too. 'The nerve of them sending this to my house.'

'I know,' I murmured, nodding.

'And they're trying to turn my parents against me.' He screwed the card up into a tiny ball. 'Do you think Tanya did this?'

'I wouldn't be a bit surprised.'

'There are probably others in this too.' He gave a grim smile. 'Well, they'll be sorry.'

He marched off and got my coat, then walked me back to my house. It was dark and windy, but there was a handful of silver stars glittering in the sky. They looked like eyes – friendly eyes – staring down on us.

'Look,' I said to Aidan.

He glanced up but hardly seemed to notice them. He was lost in thought. Then he suddenly announced. ' I know what I'm going to do.'

'What?'

'I'll put the picture in Tanya's bag tomorrow as planned. But the next day I'll deliver six more hits.'

'Six!' I exclaimed.

'That's right. I'll put my pictures in six more bags – any six, I don't care.'

'Oh, but that's a bit unfair,' I said. 'You

could be sending a picture to someone who's had nothing to do with this. Like poor Alison, for instance.'

'I'm punishing the whole class,' replied Aidan, sounding like a teacher now. 'They won't dare send any more cards to my house after that. I'm going to start on the pictures tonight.'

He left me at the top of my road. I was getting more and more uneasy. Sending out all those pictures wasn't right. But there was no talking to Aidan at the moment. He was too upset and worked-up. Maybe tomorrow, when he'd calmed down and was away from that attic.

I arrived at my house. I opened the little gate, then turned round to shut it. But there was no need. The gate was creeping shut all by itself. It's the wind, I thought. I touched the gate. And then I felt something pressing it from the other side.

I fled into the house, my heart thumping wildly.

The Frighteners hadn't gone away at all.

They were still stalking me.

Chapter Fourteen

'Of course the Frighteners have gone. You saw me taking the spell off you,' Aidan said crossly. We were whispering to each other at the start of school.

'But I felt them pushing against my gate. And I know it was them.'

'Chloe, do you trust me?' Aidan was looking directly at me.

'Yes, of course I do.'

'Well, the Frighteners have gone. You were just imagining it.'

'Stop all this talking now,' said Mr Karr, glancing at Aidan and me.

There was silence for a while, then Aidan whispered. 'I'm going ahead with the "hit" at breaktime.' It was strange to hear Aidan talking like a character from a gangster film. It didn't really suit him. 'You know what you've got to do,' he said.

'Yes,' I replied unenthusiastically.

Aidan gave me one of his piercing stares. 'You won't let me down, will you, Chloe?' Well, when a friend says that — it's just as if they're blackmailing you. And you can't refuse. But what Aidan was doing felt all wrong to me.

At the start of break Aidan whispered, 'Here we go.' We followed Tanya down the corridor and over to the pegs. I watched her put her bag down. It was really flash and expensive. Typical of her.

Now I had to distract Tanya's attention. How was I going to do that? I hadn't planned this out at all. I saw Aidan hovering. I must think of something quickly.

Then, to my total surprise Tanya came up to me. 'Can I talk to you?' she asked.

This was a piece of luck. 'Yes, sure.'

She nodded at me to follow her outside. Better and better. Then she half-pulled me over to the side of the playground. Tom was lurking there. I became suspicious.

'Just so you know,' Tanya said to me, 'I've told my brother, Rupert, about Aidan's stupid pictures. He's fifteen,' she added.

'But how totally fascinating,' I said.

'My brother says it's all a hoax,' Tanya went on.

'You've got nothing to worry about then, have you?' I replied.

'My brother says Aidan's got to stop doing all this.'

'Your brother says a lot, doesn't he. By the way, did you put a letter through Aidan's door last night?' I asked.

'I don't know what you're talking about,' said Tanya.

But I knew she did.

'Just tell Aidan he's got to stop doing all this,' she cried.

'Tell him yourself,' I replied.

'I don't know why Aidan's being so nasty,' she went on.

That's when something in me snapped. 'Don't you? I suppose you've never been nasty to him, have you?'

Tanya looked blankly at me.

'For a start, there was that open evening when you were so rude about his mum and dad: going on about how ancient they were. They heard every word you said, you know.'

'I don't remember anything about that,' said Tanya quickly. 'Aidan's made up the whole thing.'

She was being so annoying I wanted to smack her. Actually, if anyone deserved a picture in their bag it was Tanya. I wondered if Aidan had done the hit yet.

Tanya sighed loudly. 'Well, I'm sorry, Tom, but she just won't help.'

Tom had been leaning against the wall watching us intently but not saying a thing. Then he turned to me. 'The Frighteners came back last night, you know.'

'Are you sure?' I began.

'I woke up and there was one sitting on my chair.'

'Maybe it was just a dream,' I suggested.

'No, because I went over to it and it stared right back at me.' His voice rose and rose. 'It started hissing and spitting as if I were its worst enemy.'

'I'd have screamed the whole house

down if I'd seen it,' cried Tanya.

'And then it just vanished away again,' continued Tom, 'but I couldn't stop shivering for hours because it's such a horrible thing. Well, you've seen them, Chloe?'

'Yes,' I murmured.

'Do you still see them?' he asked.

I hesitated.

'You do, don't you?' he cried. 'Aidan hasn't taken the spell off us at all.'

'Of course, he hasn't,' interrupted Tanya.

'Yes, he has,' I said. 'I saw him do it.'

'So why are they still coming back then?' demanded Tom.

'I'm not sure,' I replied, weakly.

In the distance the bell was being rung. 'Come on, Tom, we're just wasting our time here,' yelled Tanya.

She marched off into school but to my surprise, Tom didn't go after her. 'Actually,' he said quietly, 'I do remember

making up those jokes about Aidan's mum and dad. It was only supposed to be a laugh but . . .' He paused for a moment. 'In the back of your mind you know something's wrong but somehow you just carry on doing it, don't you?'

I nodded.

'But I had no idea they could hear me. That's the truth, Chloe. And it's not much good saying it now, but I am truly sorry.' His face was all crunched up. He looked as if he was trying very hard not to cry.

That's why I blurted out, 'It'll be all right, and the Frighteners will go. I'll make sure of that.'

I didn't know what I was talking about really. How could I make sure the Frighteners would go? But I just wanted to cheer him up. Well, I did that all right. He must have thanked me about fourteen times before he ran off.

I walked slowly into school, lost in thought. Then I spotted Aidan. He gave me the thumbs-up. So he'd planted the picture in Tanya's bag.

Well, that would teach her I suppose. I wondered whereabouts Aidan had hidden the picture. Perhaps it would be in her story file. We were writing our stories next. Yes, that would be a good place. And she just had to take one glance at the Frighteners for the spell to work.

One glance, and she would be haunted. A shudder ran through me.

I walked into the classroom. Aidan was already sitting at his desk. Tanya was boasting loudly to this other girl about where she was going this weekend. And she was laughing, quite unaware of the terrible shock awaiting her. Now she was reaching down to open her bag.

I turned away. I didn't want to watch. To be honest, I hated being involved in this. I wish Aidan had just done the hit without telling me. Instead, I was a part of it, an accomplice.

And really, no-one should be terrorised by the Frighteners. Not even Tanya. It wasn't right. But what could I do? I remembered something Tom had said. 'In the back of your mind you know something's wrong but you just carry on doing it.'

Or sometimes you don't do anything to stop it.

Any moment now I'd hear Tanya let out one almighty shriek. I waited. This was agony. And then a voice yelled out, 'Tanya, don't open that bag!' There was a buzz of surprise. I was quite surprised too. The words just seemed to escape from my lips.

I whirled round. Tanya gazed at me. She knew instantly what had happened. All the colour had drained from her face.

'Is it in my bag now?' she shrilled.

'Yes.'

I caught a glimpse of Aidan and wished I hadn't. He just looked so shocked as if he couldn't believe what I'd done. Now I felt all knotted up inside.

'Where . . . where is it in my bag?' asked Tanya, stuttering now.

'I don't know,' I replied.

'But I've only got to see the picture and . . .' her voice fell away. Her hands were starting to shake.

The rest of the class was murmuring sympathetically but no-one was getting especially close to her.

'Ask Mr Karr to take it out,' called someone.

Then all at once I had an idea. 'Follow

me,' I said to Tanya. 'And bring your bag with you.'

'Yes, all right,' she whispered.

'If Mr Karr wants us we won't be long,' I said, to no-one in particular.

Then we rushed down the corridor. 'Are we going to see the Headmistress?' she asked.

'No, we're going to the girls' loo,' I replied.

'What!' she stopped. 'Why on earth are we going there?'

'Just follow me and stop squawking,' I said.

And amazingly, she did.

We walked inside the girls' loo. Nobody else was around. I went and stood in front of the large mirror above the basins. Next I beckoned her to stand beside me.

'What are we doing here?' she cried.

'Listen and you'll find out. Now, I'll hold your bag for you while you take everything out of it.'

She gasped. 'No.'

'But all the time I want you to keep looking in that mirror. Don't stop staring into it for a second. I'm sure that won't be hard for you,' I added under my breath.

'But why?' she asked.

'Because, for the spell to work you have to see the picture, don't you?'

'Yes.'

'Well, you won't see the picture. You'll only be looking at its reflection.'

Tanya considered this for a moment. 'But that's really clever.'

'I know. So hurry up before Mr Karr sends a search party for us. I've got hold of the bag so you start taking things out.'

Tanya reached forward. She stopped. 'I'm not sure I can do this,' she said in a small frightened voice.

'Oh yes, you can,' I replied, 'and provided you don't look away from the mirror you'll be perfectly safe.'

Tanya pulled out her story folder, giving a little gasp as she did so. 'I bet he's put it in here,' she said.

'Keep your eyes fixed ahead,' I urged.

Tanya opened the folder. 'Nothing,' she whispered.

She went through everything else in her bag until only one thing was left. A disgustingly bright, pink lunch box. Just looking at it gave me a rash. 'He wouldn't have put it in there, would he?' said Tanya.

'I think he must have.'

She opened it very carefully then jolted as if she'd just received an electric shock. 'It's there all right.'

'OK, just stay cool,' I murmured. 'Now, take the picture out and keep holding it up to the mirror.' I was trying to sound calm but in the mirror sweat was glistening all over my forehead.

In a kind of slow motion Tanya brought the picture out then let her lunch box fall to the floor. She was shaking from head to toe.

'You've done really well,' I said. 'Now, fold it over and pass it to me.'

Moments later I was holding the picture. I stared down at the two words on the back of it. 'The Frighteners.' I'd never have thought two words could make my skin creep so much.

Tanya was right beside me, breathing so fast she sounded as if she'd just run down a mountain.

'You're safe,' I said.

She let out a great sigh of relief.

'I feel as if we've just defused a bomb,' I whispered.

She nodded. Then she swallowed hard and screwed her face up. I thought she was going to be sick. Instead, she gulped and said, 'And I'm truly sorry for all the things I've said about you.'

I stared at her. 'You're not actually apologising to me, are you? Quick, where's my diary!'

Her lips twitched. She was practically smiling. 'At first I thought you were the rudest, most big-headed girl I'd ever met,' she said, 'but you're just different, aren't you?'

Before I could reply she'd picked up her bag and linked arms with me. To my embarrassment we walked back into class together.

Aidan turned his head away when I sat down. I knew he thought I'd betrayed him.

I had to make him understand why I'd helped Tanya.

I waited until the end of the lesson.

Then I gave him back the picture and said, 'I'm sorry, Aidan, but you can't do this to people. And those Frighteners aren't obeying you. Tom's still . . .'

'I did it all for you.' He fired the words at me, then walked away. He wouldn't listen to anything else I said, just acted as if I wasn't there.

I stared at him in frustration. I couldn't talk to him here. And tonight he'd shut himself away in that attic plotting his next hits, with only the Frighteners for company.

What kind of life was that?

He deserved so much better. He was, actually, a very interesting person. The rest of the class wouldn't believe that. But they'd never bothered to get to know him. Only I really knew him. That's why I had to help Aidan now.

But how?

If only I could pull him out of that terrible room and away from the shell.

For Aidan wasn't just putting spells on other people, he was under a spell too. And while the shell was there I couldn't break it.

After school I tried to talk to him again. He turned to me for a moment, his face a mask. Then he rushed off. His mum was waiting at the gates for him in a taxi. Then I remembered why. Of course, he had to go to the dentist.

And that gave me an idea. It shivered in my head. I could never do that.

But if I wanted to save Aidan I had no choice.

Chapter Fifteen

I ran all the way to Aidan's house. The wind raced alongside me, whistling and moaning in my ear. I had to stop and catch my breath before I rang on Aidan's doorbell.

I stood waiting for Aidan's dad to answer. If he wasn't in, then my whole plan was sunk. It was such a simple idea really: that shell seemed to have Aidan hypnotised. But if I took the shell out of the attic, would that break the spell and let Aidan be himself again? I was about to find out because I could hear slow footsteps.

His dad opened the door and looked pleased to see me. 'Well, hello Chloe. This is a nice surprise. Unfortunately Aidan's at the dreaded dentist at the moment. But you are very welcome to come in and wait for him. I've just made a pot of tea . . .'

'Actually,' I interrupted, 'why I called round was — well I think I left something behind in the attic yesterday and I wondered if I might just go and look for it.'

'But of course my dear. What was it you left behind?'

My mind jammed. I couldn't think. 'A pencil,' I said, lamely. 'It's quite a special one,' I added.

'Well, Aidan won't be long. So he could pop up and get it for you.'

'No,' I practically shouted. 'It's all right, I'll get it,' I added more calmly.

But then Aidan's dad raised his hand. 'You have just reminded me. I've got a gift for your father.'

'You have!' I exclaimed.

'Oh, it's just a small thing. Come inside, dear, while I find it.'

Before I could say anything he'd shuffled off. I had no choice but to follow him into the kitchen. I glanced at my watch. I didn't have a second to waste. I'd just grab my dad's present and bolt upstairs.

Most of the kitchen was taken up by an ancient-looking table. It was covered with papers and books, while bang in the middle was a long, green vase brimming with fresh flowers.

'Sit down, my dear,' he said. 'Make yourself at home. Now, I'm sure I saw your father's gift here.' He started rifling through the stuff on the table. 'No, it's not there. Ah, the tea should be brewed now.'

He poured the tea from a teapot covered in a knitted, blue cosy with a bobble on the top. I smothered a giggle. Then I noticed he was pouring out two cups. He pushed aside some of the papers on the table.

'There we are Chloe, dear,' he said. 'That will warm you up.' He seemed to have quite forgotten I wasn't having any tea and I was too polite to tell him.

He sat down opposite me. 'I just want you to know how pleased we are that Aidan has found himself such a good friend.'

Perched on the edge of a chair, I smiled faintly at him. I liked Aidan's dad very much. But he couldn't have picked a worse moment for a little chat.

'Aidan has never mentioned anyone from school before. And we know he's spent a good deal of time on his own. So we're . . .'

Suddenly the front door rattled. I started in alarm. 'Here they are,' said Aidan's dad. He smiled at me. 'Just in time for tea, aren't they.'

He ambled to the door. While I felt a huge stab of disappointment. So my plan had failed. And now I was going to have to face Aidan, who'd be most suspicious about me turning up here at this time.

I waited for Aidan's voice and that of his mum. Instead there was silence save for Aidan's dad. He gave a brief laugh. Then he came in waving a newspaper. 'Just the local rag, early for once.'

Inside my head I let out a huge sigh of relief. But I had to move fast. 'Now, I really must go and get my pencil,' I said, as firmly as I could.

'All right dear. Finish your tea while I get your father's gift. I think I must have left it in the sitting room.'

As soon as he'd gone I leapt up and

132

poured all my tea down the sink. Then I waited impatiently for Aidan's dad. He was ages. At last he came back panting slightly and waving a copy of the book he'd written, 'A WARTIME SCREEN. BRITISH CINEMA 1939—1945.' He glanced at my empty cup.

'My, you were thirsty, weren't you. Would you like another . . .'

'No, no,' I said hastily.

He handed me the book.

'That's really kind of you,' I cried. 'My dad will treasure this.'

He was beaming now. 'Do you think he would like me to sign it?'

I couldn't say no, could I? He took the book back. But of course he didn't have a pen. And then he found one which didn't work. So he had to search for another one while I waited, bristling with impatience.

At last, with the signed book under my arm I darted into the hall.

'Put it on the hall table if you like and pick it up when you go,' he said.

'Thanks,' I replied, leaving the book where he'd suggested.

'Now, are you sure you don't want to wait for Aidan? He'll be home any minute.'

'No thanks,' I said hastily, sprinting up the stairs.

'Well, take care going up those steps, won't you?'

'I will.' I was already climbing the twisty steps leading into the attic.

I clambered inside. There was a blind over the little window. And it took my eyes a few seconds to get used to the gloom. Darkness hung over this room like a mist.

All at once I had the feeling that I wasn't alone. Was one of the Frighteners hiding in a shadowy corner? Then I told myself that was impossible. The

Frighteners could only drop in when the brick was removed.

Still, my legs were like jelly as I walked over to the wall. Every one of my footsteps seemed to echo around the attic. I immediately spotted the loose brick. I took a deep breath and moved it away. And there it was. The shell.

My heart started performing this strange drumbeat. I really didn't want to pick it up. I certainly didn't want to take it home. Where would I keep it for a start? Not in my bedroom, that's for sure. It would have to be out in the shed. That was for later anyhow. Right now I just had to take the thing and get out of here fast.

So I snatched it up. I was, actually, holding the shell. My eyes roved around nervously. All those animals on the wall made me feel as if I was in a dark forest.

And then I saw a flicker of movement. It was the picture of the tiger. It was trembling and stirring. I gaped at it, horrified. I could hear it rustling softly, just as if it were whispering to itself.

The picture was slowly coming to life. Any moment now that tiger would swoop down off the wall and ... Now I was really frightening myself. And if I let myself become frightened I was finished.

'It's just the wind making the pictures move, that's all,' I told myself over and over. Then I looked away from the wall and went over to Aidan's table. On it was a pile of pictures. They were turned upside down and on the back of the top one was written, THE FRIGHTENERS. I bet they were all ready for tomorrow. Aidan's next strike against six unfortunate pupils.

He was like a general drawing up plans for his troops. I imagined him telling the Frighteners about their next assignment. Only Aidan wasn't at war with a particular country, he was at war with everyone.

Still, if the shell was missing Aidan couldn't go ahead. I gripped it tightly. Aidan would be so angry when he discovered his precious shell had gone. He'd come marching round to my house right away. There'd be a really, terrible scene. But in the end it would be worth it if . . . my plan just had to work.

I checked my watch. Six precious minutes had passed. I must leave. But then I remembered I hadn't put the brick back. That meant I'd left the Frighteners' entrance open. Why, one of them could sneak in here at any moment.

I raced across that attic like a frightened deer and took a quick glance inside the hole. Two purple eyes stared back at me.

I nearly fell over with shock. What should I do? But there was no time to do anything. There was a quiver of movement by my feet. Something flitted past. When I looked down it had vanished.

It had just wanted me to know it was here. Aidan said the Frighteners could appear and disappear in the blink of an eye. Now it was watching and waiting for another chance to terrify me.

The air seemed to have gone chilly all at once. Aidan told me that was a sign a Frightener was close by. Any moment now it would materialize again, perhaps from that corner over there. That was the darkest part of the room.

And that's exactly what happened. One of the Frighteners rose up out of the shadows like a genie coming out of a bottle. I was too stunned to move. All the hair on my head was standing up like bristles.

Could I hear something too? Yes, I was sure I could. Its wings beating very slowly.

'Leave me alone!' I screamed. I spotted a pile of books. I picked up the fattest one and lobbed it at the Frightener. The book bounced against the wall, then landed on the ground with a heavy thump. But it hadn't touched the Frightener which had just melted into the gloom.

And throwing that book was so stupid. All I'd done was make the Frightener even angrier than it had been before. Now it was hiding somewhere, getting ready to strike again. Only this time it would make straight for me and its vast jaws would spring open . . .

There was a sudden iciness in the air. If I turned round I'd see it right beside me, getting ready to attack.

'Get away,' I screamed, raising my hand as if to ward it off. All at once I lost my grip on the shell. It slipped out of my hand and went spinning across the attic floor. I stood there trembling. What should I do now? That was dead easy. Charge out of here as fast as possible.

Yet I had to take the shell with me.

It was lying right by the doorway. I edged over to it. I crouched down. I knew I was being watched. And if I picked up the shell the Frightener would spring out of the shadows again.

I had to try, though. I let my hand crawl nearer. I stretched out a finger. I held it again. I ran my fingers over it. Now I should speed away. But then I had another idea.

Why didn't I just crush the shell? I could stand on it right now. There'd be a nasty crunching noise but afterwards it would be destroyed for good.

I hesitated. I had to think about this a bit more.

And then I felt a rush of cold air in front of me. It was as if the Frighteners had read my thoughts. One of them would be in the doorway now, its tail thrashing furiously like a demented guard dog.

I slowly twisted up my head.

A dark silhouette rose from the doorway and said. 'The Frighteners will never let you take my shell away.'

Chapter Sixteen

It was Aidan.

I shrank back, flushing guiltily. He grabbed the shell from me. Then he cradled it in his arms as if it were a tiny creature.

'You're just like all the rest, aren't you,' he said, bitterly. 'And now you're trying to steal my shell.'

'I wasn't trying to steal it,' I cried. 'I was rescuing you.'

Aidan gave a nasty, high-pitched laugh.

'It's true, Aidan.' I went on talking really fast. 'This shell might be magic but it's bad magic. And it's put a bad spell on you.'

He laughed again. 'You just wanted it

141

for yourself. You'd have got it too if it hadn't been for my Frighteners.'

Aidan's mum suddenly called from downstairs. 'Chloe, would you like to stay for a meal, dear? You'd be very welcome.'

Aidan answered for me. 'It's all right, Mum, Chloe's just leaving.' Then he added in a much lower voice. 'And she won't be coming back, ever.'

'All right,' I said, wearily. 'If that's how you want it.'

'It is.'

I turned to go.

'And by the way, Chloe,' he said, 'you can expect a picture in your bag soon.'

'What!' I gasped, anger flooding through me now. 'That's your answer to everything, isn't it. Someone does something you don't like and hey presto, they get a picture in their bag. And no-one must ever disagree with the great Aidan, must they? Well, go on, put six drawings in my bag. Set them all on me. And you can sit up here for the rest of your life drawing monsters. I just don't care.'

Then I pounded down those steps and stormed out of the house. I could feel the anger spinning round and round in my head. And my eyes stung as if I'd left soap in them.

The nerve of him threatening me with the Frighteners. Well, I'd finished with Aidan for evermore. He just didn't deserve me.

Outside it was beginning to get dark and the night was turning wild. The wind roared and raged, blowing rain into my face. It sounded as angry as I felt. No-one seemed to be about. A few cars whizzed by. And a dog barked. I thought longingly of Harvey. He'd be wondering where I was. I couldn't wait to get home.

I was nearly at the top of my road. Already the houses were glittering with lights. Everyone was inside. And soon that's where I would be too. I was never going to help Aidan again. Just thinking his name made me grit my teeth with fury.

I looked ahead of me.

And then I saw something which turned my blood cold.

Chapter Seventeen

Without any warning or sound they had appeared.

And now they were waiting at the top of my road for me.

The Frighteners.

There were three of them ranged in front of me like a supernatural roadblock. Aidan had obviously sent them. He'd whispered into that shell, 'Stop Chloe getting into her own house.' That was so nasty of him.

I was scared and angry and on the verge of crying.

But mainly I was scared.

What could I do, call out, get someone?

I turned and peered into the nearest

garden. It was very neat and tidy, with even all the leaves brushed into a corner. I had spoken to the woman who lived there. Now she always waved to me when I went past. Should I go in and get her help? But what could I say?

'Oh hello, there's this band of ghostly monsters stopping me getting into my house. Would you please tell them off and make them fly back home to their master.' She'd think I was just trying to be funny. And would she even be able to see the Frighteners? The audience in the cinema certainly never saw them.

Perhaps only the person who's being haunted – and Aidan of course – can see them.

Still, I wished another human being was at least around.

I glanced hopefully into the garden again. There was no-one about. But then came a sound which made my spine creep. A terrible screeching noise. Moments later I heard it again. Was it the Frighteners? Or was it just a cat somewhere? I didn't know.

I couldn't see anything.

A bird called. Wherever it was it sounded lonely and lost. And then I watched something gliding down out of the sky, like a ghostly parachutist. I recognized it at once.

It landed at the top of the cherry tree. I stared at the tree in mounting horror. Any moment now it will come swooping down on me. I could try and run. But if I did I'd only meet those other Frighteners. And anyway, I was so tired of running.

So let the Frightener do its worst. Let it sink its fangs into my body. All at once I was too weary and fed-up to care.

I didn't want to see it attacking me, though. So I screwed my eyes up tight and waited breathlessly. I began to shiver. It had grown very cold. A coldness which seemed to be reaching out for me.

Any moment the Frightener would strike. I swallowed and waited and felt numb with terror. I could hear it now hissing louder than a hive full of bees. But still, nothing happened. And this waiting was just agony.

Suddenly my knees started trembling. To steady myself I grabbed out blindly for some kind of support. My hand felt an icy draught. With a flash of fear I realized what I'd done. I'd actually touched one of the Frighteners. And my hand had gone right through it. It was just like touching smoke or a cloud (not that I've ever touched a cloud). There was nothing to it really.

My eyes flew open. Nothing seemed to be there. I blinked, and there it was again, hovering just in front of me. But it seemed wispy and faint. I took a deep breath and tapped it very lightly. I felt a tiny breeze but that was all. I hit it again, only much harder. And this time I swished it right away from me, just as if it were an old cobweb or something.

Then I sprinted towards the Frighteners at the top of my road. 'I don't believe in you,' I cried. And hey presto, they were gone. But had they ever really been there? Or were they just a product of my imagination going into overdrive?

I suddenly remembered what Dad had said to me. 'Our imagination is a wonderful amazing gift, but you've got to be careful with it. If you let it overpower you, you can scare yourself to death.' That's exactly what I'd done. Or rather, Aidan had.

Aidan, with his eerie pictures and yes . . . he's got a really, powerful mind. I'll give him that. He thinks about things so hard he makes you see them too. In fact, he practically hypnotises you.

So after I left he must have sat in the attic wishing that the Frighteners would stop me going home. They did as well, but they won't again. I've shown that my mind is just as strong as his now.

I was about to march triumphantly into my house when I had another idea. I wanted to tell Aidan that his sneaky little plan hadn't worked. And that I didn't care how many pictures he put in my bag now.

I couldn't wait to see his face when I told him that. So I tore back. His mum was outside her house chatting to another woman. She wagged a finger at me.

'I know why you've come back,' she said.

I started. 'You do?'

'Forgot your dad's book, didn't you?'

I smiled with relief. 'That's it,' I replied. 'And I just wanted to tell Aidan something too.'

'He's still upstairs in the attic. So go right up, dear.'

Aidan's parents were so nice. I'd miss them. But not Aidan. I just had one thing to say to him. Then I was out of here, never to return.

I climbed into the attic. Darkness had settled on this room like a giant bat. The blackness was so thick I could hardly see anything at first.

But right away something felt wrong.

And then I realized what it was.

I couldn't see Aidan.

He had vanished.

Chapter Eighteen

Where was he? He must be here. Unless he had crept downstairs without his mum noticing. Then, deep in the shadows a movement caught my eye. At first I thought it was one of the Frighteners.

But then I looked closer and saw Aidan. He was all hunched up in the corner with both hands clutching the shell. His eyes were shut and he was biting his lip.

'Aidan,' I whispered, frantically.

His eyes sprang open and he made a faint noise in his throat like a startled animal.

Seeing him sent all my anger flooding back. 'How dare you send the Frighteners after me. How dare you!'

'What!'

'Don't deny it. I saw them, three of them blocking the way to my house. That was such a cute idea. But you see, I accidentally put my hand through one of them, so now I know they're nothing, really. Nothing at all.'

Aidan's eyes widened in shock. 'I don't know what you're talking about. I never sent the Frighteners after you. Honestly.'

I shook my head. 'Well, then they must have come charging after me just for the fun of it. They're totally out of control.' I stopped. I gazed down at him. 'Why are you sitting in the corner like that? You look as if you're playing hide and seek.'

He stared down at his shell. 'Just been wishing I could disappear, that's all.'

'What!'

'I've been wishing just as hard as I could. I even imagined I was starting to vanish.'

I thought back to when I'd first come in. For a few seconds I really hadn't been able to see Aidan. Could he have actually disappeared for a moment? Or had he just been camouflaged by the darkness. It was so hard to know what was real and what was imagination in this room.

'But why did you want to disappear?' I demanded.

'I was so ashamed about what I'd said to you. How could I have threatened to put a picture in your bag. I don't know what made me say it. But I knew I'd ruined everything with you, my only friend. So I wanted to disappear. I wish I had, too.'

'Now you're just feeling sorry for yourself,' I snapped.

'No I'm not.'

'Yes you are. It's your victims you should be feeling sorry for.'

He looked up at me. 'I know. But I would never really put a picture in your bag. And I didn't tell the Frighteners to follow you home either, I swear on my life, I didn't, Chloe.'

I crouched down beside him. 'All right, calm down, I believe you. And I'm glad you didn't disappear, though don't ask me why. But you can't leave the Frighteners rampaging about. I don't believe in them any more. And if one came near me I'd just swat it away like a fly, but everyone else in our school still believes in them.'

'I know.' He slowly got to his feet. He put the shell in his pocket, then went over and picked up the six pictures of the

152

Frighteners he'd prepared for tomorrow.

He ran his fingers over them as if he were holding something very valuable. But then he began ripping them up into tinier and tinier pieces. They fell like tiny, dark leaves on to the floor. Around us the pictures on the wall rustled and trembled as if fearful they would be next.

Suddenly Aidan was looking directly at me. 'I should let the Frighteners go, shouldn't I?'

'Yes, you should,' I agreed, firmly.

He gave a strange, little laugh. 'It's hard, though, because the Frighteners – well, they're the only bit of power I've ever had.'

'But you got that power by scaring people half to death and that isn't right, is it?'

'I know, I know,' he said, almost impatiently.

Then I added a bit more gently. 'Look, the Frighteners are just imaginary, fictional. But you still created them. And you made people like Tom – and me for a while – believe in them. So now you've got to write them out of our lives. You've got to get rid of them, once and for all.'

Without another word Aidan picked up the shell. 'I'm going to summon them for one last meeting.'

Perhaps because I didn't believe in them any more I never saw them assemble into the attic. But Aidan assured me they were all here. For a moment I thought I heard one of them hissing. But then I decided it was just the wind.

Aidan began speaking to them. He spoke very quietly and gently. He said he was setting them free.

'They're really frightened,' said Aidan to me. 'Can you hear them?'

'No, I can't. And anyway, they're only getting a taste of their own medicine,' I said quickly.

Aidan shook his head. 'It was my fault. I taught them to enjoy scaring people. I put them on the wrong path. I don't deserve them,' he said sadly.

Then he added. 'Chloe, I've just had a crazy thought. When the Frighteners stopped you going home, you don't think it was because they wanted you to come back here?'

'How do you mean?' I asked.

'Well, they knew I was unhappy and that I was missing you. So they decided to bring you back. How do they do that? Well, they only know one way: by scaring you back here, of course. What do you think?'

'Oh, I don't know,' I began. But then I started in surprise. I was sure I'd heard one of the Frighteners cry out and it sounded just as terrified as Aidan had said. I looked around and then, right in the furthest corner I glimpsed a pair of very dim, purple eyes.

They stared eerily back at me.

I shook my head. The image vanished instantly. What I'd just seen wasn't real. It was only that Aidan believes in the Frighteners so strongly he makes me see them too. He's like a very good story-teller who plants pictures inside your head. And you think about those pictures so much they become real, and even seem to have a life of their own.

'Aidan, your theory about the Frighteners bringing me back here to help you . . . well, you might be right. I wouldn't put anything past them.'

Aidan nodded and smiled faintly. Then he announced, in a voice that was so weak

I could hardly hear it. 'They've gone now, Chloe.'

I didn't know what to say. So in the end I just reached out and gave his hand a squeeze. He slowly reached forward and picked up the shell. 'Would you look after this for me, just in case I get lonely and try and bring them back?'

Tears were smarting against the back of my eyes now. 'Oh, you won't be lonely, Aidan. I'll see to that. But I'll look after the shell. Of course I will.'

'Thanks a lot.'

He handed the shell to me and carefully put the brick back in the wall.

He stood silent for a moment. Then he said. 'Let's get out of here, shall we?'

We went downstairs. The gift for my dad was still on the table in the hall waiting for me. And Aidan's mum called out from the kitchen that tea would be ready in five minutes.

'Make it ten, Mum, please,' called back Aidan. 'I want to walk Chloe back.'

Outside the twilight was deepening. I looked around me and then I froze in horror. Just beside Aidan's feet loomed a dark shape.

Then it started to move.

Chapter Nineteen

I gaped at the dark figure. It gave a great echoing bark, then it started running around in circles. I let out a huge whistle of relief.

'Harvey,' I cried. 'Did you slip out to find me? He does that sometimes, you know.'

Harvey was wagging his tail but gazing up at Aidan.

'Oh, I see, it's Aidan you've been missing, is it?'

Straightaway, Aidan picked Harvey up. 'Have you been looking for me? What a clever dog.'

Harvey snuggled himself down in Aidan's arms. Normally I'd have felt a bit jealous. But today I was just pleased Harvey had appeared when he did.

And then came this sound, like the faraway shriek of a train. Only it sounded so miserable and scared and lonely, it also reminded me of . . .

'Do you think that's my Frighteners missing me?' whispered Aidan.

I hesitated for just a moment. 'Yes I do.'

I dug into my bag and brought out the shell. 'One last message to help them on their way.'

He nodded. Then he started talking into the shell in this really gentle reassuring voice. Harvey thought Aidan was talking to him and began licking his face. Aidan went on whispering into that shell for ages. At last he stopped. And he gazed up into the night sky just as if the Frighteners were heading towards the stars now. Perhaps they were.

'I think they heard me,' he said. And he

smiled as if he was just waking up from a wonderful dream. He gave me the shell again. 'Now don't try and conjure them back, will you.'

'No fear,' I cried. 'But anyway, I don't think I could. This shell won't work for me, or anyone else either. Only you can create charmers like the Frighteners, because you're . . .'

'Mad!'

'Yeah, you're mad all right. But you haven't just got blood in your veins — there's magic pumping around there too.'

He looked startled. 'Really!'

'I think you've got much more to discover about yourself and this magic-thinking you were telling me about. In fact, I would say you've hardly started.'

A light flared in his eyes. 'You might be right.'

'Of course I'm right. And I bet one day I'll be boasting how I knew that world-famous magician, sorcerer and general spellmaster, Aidan Grant.'

We'd reached the top of my road. Aidan put Harvey gently down on the ground and I packed the shell in my bag again. As I was going Aidan called after me. 'Chloe, you don't mind taking the shell, do you?'

I didn't answer for a moment. Then I smiled into the darkness. 'No, because now it's a gift. A gift from a friend.'

THE END